A Dog's Heart

Mikhail Bulgakov

Translated by Antonina W. Bouis

ALMA CLASSICS LTD
3 Castle Yard
Richmond
Surrey TW10 6TF
United Kingdom
www.almaclassics.com

Sobach'e Serdtse first published in Russian in 1987
© by the Estate of Mikhail Bulgakov
This translation first published by Alma Classics Ltd (previously
Oneworld Classics Ltd) in 2011
This new edition published by Alma Classics Ltd in 2016

Translation and Notes © Antonina W. Bouis, 2011

Cover design: nathanburtondesign.com

Extra Material © Alma Classics Ltd

Printed and bound by CPI Group (UK) Ltd, Croydon, CR0 4YY

ISBN: 978-1-84749-568-6

Contents

Mikhail Bulgakov (1891–1940)

Afanasy Ivanovich Bulgakov,
Bulgakov's father

Varvara Mikhailovna Bulgakova,
Bulgakov's mother

Lyubov Belozerskaya,
Bulgakov's second wife

Yelena Shilovskaya,
Bulgakov's third wife

Москва.—Moscou. № 322.
Садовая Тріумфальная д. Пигитъ.—Sadovaya Maison ...

Bulgakov's residences on Bolshaya Sadovaya St. (above) and Nashchokinsky
Pereulok (bottom left); an unfinished letter to Stalin (bottom right)

An autograph page from *The Master and Margarita*

Introduction

A Dog's Heart is a Russian Frankenstein tale with a gentle twist and a happy end. A kindly professor performs a daring experiment to turn a dog into a human being by transplanting human organs into it; the result is hilarious social satire and a condemnation of revolution and the new communist state.

Mikhail Bulgakov (1891–1940) suffered at the hands of the Soviet system. His family, educated and religious, managed to emigrate to France. As a doctor in the First World War and later during the Civil War, he could not. His life's vicissitudes made it difficult for him to survive as a writer: after performing a tracheotomy on a child in 1917 he contracted diphtheria, which he treated with morphine and soon found himself addicted. He went through three marriages and battled constantly with Soviet censorship. Partly because of the latter, his masterpiece *The Master and Margarita* was not published until 1966, and the manuscript of *A Dog's Heart* was confiscated in 1926, shortly after it was written, and not published until forty years later by a Russian-language press in Germany.

He had some successes, most notably the play *Days of the Turbins* (1926), based on his novel *The White Guard* (1924), about the family of an officer who fought against the Red Army in the civil war that tore Russia apart for years after the Bolshevik Revolution of 1917. The play was produced by Konstantin Stanislavsky at the famed Moscow Art Theatre only with the permission of Stalin, who loved it and attended almost every performance. Yet Stalin would neither allow Bulgakov to produce his play *Batum* about the dictator's youth, nor to publish any of his prose. Nor would Stalin permit Bulgakov to join his family abroad. Despair and stress exacerbated his kidney disease and the writer died in 1940.

Bulgakov's early prose included some science fiction and fantasy. The genre is an excellent medium for social satire. Often, censors do not recognize the hidden references or, perhaps, pretend not to see. Two short stories, 'Diaboliad' and 'The Fatal Eggs', were published, and Bulgakov intended the next novella to be in the same genre. Prior to submitting *A Dog's Heart* for publication, Bulgakov read the new work aloud to a small group in March 1925. Naturally, there were quite perceptive police spies in the audience. One reported that the work mocked the proletariat, rejected terror as a means of changing people and denied all the achievements of the Soviet system. It was also, he wrote, luridly pornographic, under the guise of being scientific. He concluded: "I believe that the censors will not permit its publication. But this book has been read to an audience of forty-eight people, ninety per cent of whom are themselves writers. Thus its role, its main work, has been accomplished: it has infected the writers' minds and will sharpen their quills." The novella was banned.

Professor Preobrazhensky, a "high priest of science", is a godlike character who works on the rejuvenation of the ageing rich in order to discover the secrets of life. His disdain for the Soviet regime and *Homo socialisticus* is expressed strongly and frankly, creating problems with the new Bolsheviks running his apartment building, a quartet of fervent revolutionaries blinded by ideology and stupidity.

The narrative of *A Dog's Heart* combines several points of view, often shifting at unexpected moments: it begins with the stray dog's story of misery, licking its wounds in an alley during a blizzard, watching a young woman fight her way through the storm – for a brief moment we "tune in" on her thoughts and fears. Then the dog is picked up and led away by a well-dressed bourgeois gentleman, Professor Preobrazhensky – the dog can tell proletarians from the bourgeoisie easily. The descriptions of the luxurious apartment-cum-office, the faithful assistant, Dr Bormental, the maid and the cook are all filtered through the limited understanding of the canine mind. The narrative is continued by Dr Bormental, who keeps the case notes of the historic and God-challenging operation and recovery. Then we see things from the perspective of the new man, Sharikov, as he becomes more and more Bolshevik and anti-bourgeois, more and more radical and stupid.

These intentional shifts in angle are disorienting, as are the changes in register and vocabulary. Often it is not clear at first who is speaking or what about. But a few lines later, we see what Bulgakov wants us to see.

Preobrazhensky is now a classic character, frequently quoted by Russians. Witty, acerbic, cultured and scholarly, he is full of theories about enjoying life. He delivers a wonderful lecture on how to eat and drink properly, the main rule being: do not read Soviet newspapers before meals. He represents everything the revolutionary regime wants to eradicate, just as Sharikov is the embodiment of everything that is ruining Russia in the professor's view. To him, the Soviet culture is dumbing down the country, filling people's heads with talk of equality and rebellion instead of instilling the virtues of hard work and education.

The professor has no patience with committees and regulations, and resents the attempts to turn his commodious apartment into a communal flat.

Bulgakov's tale is imbued with religious and musical symbolism and allusions. This story of the birth of a new man takes place between late December 1924 and early January 1925; that is, between Christmas Eve on the Western calendar and Christmas Eve on the Russian Orthodox calendar. The religious underpinnings appear in the proper names: "Preobrazhensky" comes from the Russian *"Preobrazheniye"* ("Transfiguration") and is a common surname among the clergy. The Arbat area where the action takes place has lanes with names like Myortvy ("Dead") and Prechistenka ("Holy"). The professor is an opera-lover, and he sings the chorus "To the Sacred Banks of the Nile" from *Aida* when he is under stress. A new production of *Aida* entered the repertory of the Bolshoi Opera Theatre in 1922. The chorus is sung to strengthen the resolve of the Egyptian army and to aid the warrior Radames in his quest to transform the simple slave girl Aida into his legitimate wife when he becomes a commander. The first encounter with the opera is in the story's opening pages, when the stray dog grumbles about "the old biddy who sings in the moonlight – 'Celeste Aida'" (that is, "Heavenly Aida", which is Radames's love aria). When the professor is in a more cheerful mood, he likes to sing *Don Juan's Serenade*, a romance composed by Tchaikovsky to a poem by Alexei Tolstoy. In it, Don Juan entreats the lovely Nisetta to come out on her balcony so that he can play his guitar for her.

A *Dog's Heart* is incredibly accurate about Moscow in those two weeks: the references to the playbills, the circus acts listed in the newspaper, the performance of the opera and the weather are exactly right, almost as in a diary.

Many of the characters are recognizable as well. The prototype for the professor is Bulgakov's uncle, a professor of medicine and a gynaecologist. Some of Preobrazhensky's patients were well-known to readers at the time: Moritz (the young lover of a woman seeking rejuvenation) was a man-about-town whose many affairs were grist for the gossip mill; the political official with a predilection for young women was recognizable and the censors first deleted all reference to him before banning the work completely.

The "new man" created by the professor is a parody of the "new man" meant to evolve under the Soviet system. Sharikov becomes a monster who turns on his creator under the influence of socialist propaganda; frighteningly, it becomes clear that Sharikov is bound to turn on his revolutionary teachers as well. A terrible force is unleashed.

Thus, A *Dog's Heart* deftly combines reality and fact with fiction and fantasy. The main hero, the mutt Sharik, becomes the main villain, the upstart Sharikov. Full of remorse, Professor Preobrazhensky takes it upon himself to play God once again and reverses the operation. Peace is restored to the apartment, but the social experiment outside his windows continued until the end of the twentieth century.

– Antonina W. Bouis, 2011

A Dog's Heart

A Monstrous Story

Chapter 1

Aooooo-ooow-ooow! O, look at me, I'm dying! The blizzard in the alley is roaring a dirge for me, and I'm howling with it. I'm done for, gone! The bastard in the filthy cap – the cook in the normalized nutrition canteen serving the Central Economic Council – sloshed boiling water at me and burned my left side. What a creep, and a proletarian to boot! Lord, God almighty, it hurts! The boiling water ate through to the bone. So I howl and howl and howl, but how can howling help?

What did I ever do to him? What? Did he think I'd eat the Economic Council out of its stores if I rummaged in the rubbish? Greedy creature. Take a look at his mug some time: fat, broad cheeks. He's a brass-faced thief. People, help! The white-hat gave me a taste of boiling water at noon; now it's dark, around four in the afternoon, going by the onion smell from the Prechistenka fire station. The firemen get buckwheat groats for dinner, as you well know. But that's way down on my list, like mushrooms. Dogs I know from Prechistenka told me, however, that there's a place called The Bar on Neglinny Street, where people gobble up the special of the day, mushrooms *en sauce piquante*, at three roubles seventy-five a portion. To each his own – for me it's like licking galoshes… Oooow… My side is killing me, and I can see my future career absolutely clearly: tomorrow there will be sores and I'd like to know how I'm supposed to treat them. In the summer you can go down to Sokolniki Park, there's a particularly good grass there, and besides which, you can stuff yourself with sausage ends and the citizenry litter the place with greasy wrapping paper that's good to lick. And if not for some old biddy who sings in the moonlight – 'Celeste Aida'* – in a way that turns your stomach, all would be fine. But now where am I supposed to go? Have you been kicked by boots? Yes. Have you ever got a brick in the ribs? Plenty of times. I've suffered it all, I've accepted my fate, and if I'm crying now it's only from the physical pain and the hunger, because my spirit hasn't dimmed yet... The canine spirit is very tenacious. But my body is broken, battered, people have had their fun with it. The worst part is this: once he'd poured the boiling water on me, it ate through the fur, and now there's no protection for my left side. I could easily get pneumonia, and if I do, citizens, I will starve to death. When you have pneumonia, you're supposed to lie under the main stairs inside, and who's going to run around the bins in search of food except me, a bedridden bachelor dog? If my lung is affected, I'll be crawling on my belly, weakened, and any guy with a stick can finish me off. And then the street-cleaners with their badges will grab me by my legs and toss me into their cart...

Of all the proletarians, street-cleaners are the vilest scum. Human dregs, the lowest category. You get different kinds of cooks. Take the late Vlas from Prechistenka. How many lives he saved! The most important thing when you're sick is to get a bite. And there were times, the old hounds say, when Vlas would toss a bone and it would have an ounce of meat on it. May he rest in peace for being a real human being, the personal chef to the Count Tolstoys, and not from the Council of Normalized Nutrition. What they do in the name of normalized nutrition is beyond a dog's mind to understand! Those bastards use rotten corned beef to make cabbage soup, and the poor customers know nothing about it. They come, eat, guzzle it down!

This little typist of the ninth rank earns forty-five roubles but, of course, her lover gives her fine cotton stockings. And how much she has to put up with for those *fil de Perse* stockings! He doesn't just take her the usual way, he makes her do it French style. Real bastards, those French, just between you and me. Though they eat well, all washed down with red wine. Yes… So the little typist will come to eat there, she can't afford to go to The Bar on forty-five roubles! She doesn't have enough for the movies, and movies are the sole consolation for women. She shudders and winces but eats it. Just think, forty copecks for two courses, while both those courses don't even cost fifteen, because the manager steals the remaining twenty-five copecks. And is this the kind of food she should be eating? The tip of her right lung has a spot, and she has women's troubles thanks to that French stuff, they docked her wages at work and fed her putrid meat at the canteen, there she is, there she is! Running into the alley in her lover's stockings. Her feet are cold, the wind is blowing on her belly because her fur's like mine, and she wears cold undies, just a lacy appearance of underwear. Tatters for her lover. Let her try putting on flannel pants. He'll shout: "Why can't you be sexy? I'm sick and tired of my Matryona, sick of her flannel underpants, my time has come. I'm a chairman now, and everything I embezzle goes to female flesh, chocolates and bottles of Abrau-Durso!* I spent my entire youth hungry, I'm done with that, and there is no afterlife."

I pity her, I do. But I pity myself even more. That's not my egoism talking, oh no, but it's because we truly are in unequal conditions. At least she's warm at home, but what about me? Where can I go? Beaten, scalded, spat upon, where can I go? Ooooow-ooow!

"Here, boy. Sharik, come on, Sharik! Why are you whining, poor thing? Eh? Did someone hurt you?... Ooof!"

The blizzard wind, that witch, rattled the gates and smacked the young lady on the ear with its broom. It lifted her skirt to her knees, revealing creamy stockings and a narrow strip of poorly laundered lace underwear, stifling her words and sweeping away the dog.

My God, what terrible weather... Ooof... And my stomach aches. That salted meat! When will it all end?

Lowering her head, the young woman launched herself into the attack, breaking through the gates, and she was spun round and round, tossed and then twisted into a snowy funnel, before she vanished.

The dog remained near the alley, suffering the pain of his mutilated side, pressed himself against the cold wall, held his breath and decided that he would never leave this spot again, that he would die right there. Despair overwhelmed him. He felt such bitterness and pain, such loneliness and fear, that tiny canine tears bubbled from his eyes and dried on the spot. His fur on the wounded side was all in shredded, frozen clumps, revealing vicious red burns. How stupid, nasty and cruel were cooks. She called him "Sharik"...* What the hell kind of "Sharik" was he! Sharik was a fluffball, a round, well-fed, dumb, oatmeal-eating son of pedigree parents, and he was a shaggy, bony and scruffy stray, a homeless dog. But thanks for the kind thought.

The door of the brightly lit shop across the road slammed, and a citizen appeared. A citizen, not a comrade, and probably a gentleman. As he came closer, it was clear he was a gentleman. Don't you think I judge by the overcoat. Nonsense. Lots of proles wear overcoats now too. Of course, not with collars like that, no way, but still you could get confused from a distance. But I judge by the eyes – you can't mistake them either near or far! Oh, eyes are a significant thing! Like a barometer. You can see everything – who has a vast desert in his heart, who can jab you in the ribs with the toe of his boot for no reason at all, and who is afraid of everything. There's such pleasure in nipping the last type in the calf. Afraid? So there. If you're afraid, you deserve it. Grrrrr... arf!

The gentleman crossed the street confidently in the column of blowing snow and moved towards the gate. Yes, yes, I could see everything about him. He wouldn't put away that putrid corned beef, and if anyone dared serve him some he would raise such a fuss and write to the papers saying: "They gave me, Filipp Filippovich, rotten meat!"

Here he comes, closer and closer. This one eats well and doesn't steal. He won't kick you, but he's not afraid of anyone, and that's because he's never hungry. He is a gentleman who does intellectual labour, with a French pointy beard and a grey moustache, fluffy and dashing, like French knights had, but the blizzard carries his smell and it's a bad one – hospital and cigar.

What the hell brings him to the Central Economy Co-op? Now he's right there... What's he looking for? Oh-oh... What could he want to buy in that crummy little store, aren't the fancy stores on Okhotny Ryad* enough? What is it?! Sausage. Mister, if you saw how they made that sausage you wouldn't go anywhere near the store. Give it to me!

The dog mustered what little strength it had and madly crawled out from beneath the gate onto the pavement. The blizzard thundered like a rifle shot above him, billowing the huge letters on a canvas poster: "IS REJUVENATION POSSIBLE?"

Of course it is. The smell rejuvenated me, got me up off my belly, raising fiery waves in my stomach that had been empty for two days, the smell vanquished the hospital, the heavenly fragrance of ground mare with garlic and pepper.

I can smell it, I know he's got sausage in his right pocket. He's standing above me. O, master! Look at me. I am dying. We've got slaves' hearts, a miserable fate!

The dog crawled like a snake on its belly, streaming tears. Note the cook's work. But you're not going to give me any. Oh, I know rich people very well! Yet, essentially, what do you want it for? What do you want with rotten horse-meat? You won't get poison like this anywhere except at the Moscow Agricultural Processing Trust, that's for sure. You had breakfast today, you world luminary, thanks to male sex glands. Oooo-oooh… What is going on in this fair world? I guess it's too early to die, and despair is a sin. I have to lick his hands, there's nothing else left to do.

The mysterious gentleman bent over the dog, the gold frames around his eyes glinting, and took a long white package out of his right pocket. Without taking off his brown gloves, he unwrapped the paper, which the storm immediately took away, and broke off a piece of sausage, which was called Cracow Special. And gave the piece to the dog. Oh, what a selfless individual! Oooh – ooh!

"*Phweet*," the gentleman whistled and added in a stern voice, "Here! Sharik, Sharik!"

Sharik again. I've been baptized. Call me whatever you want. In return for your exceptional act...

The dog instantly pulled off the casing, clamped onto the Cracow sausage with a slurp and gulped it down in a trice. And choked on the sausage and snow to the point of tears, because he had almost swallowed the string in his greed. More, I lick your hand more. I kiss your trousers, my benefactor!

"Enough for now..." The gentleman spoke in short bursts, as if giving orders. He leant over Sharik, looked interrogatively into his eyes and unexpectedly ran his gloved hand intimately and gently over Sharik's belly.

"Ah-ha," he said portentously, "no collar, that's lovely, you're just the one I want. Follow me." He clicked his fingers. "*Phweet!*"

Follow you? To the ends of the earth. You can kick me with your suede shoes and I won't say a word.

Street lamps glowed all over Prechistenka. His side ached terribly, but Sharik sometimes forgot about it, lost in one thought only – how not to lose in the crowd the miraculous vision in a fur coat, and how to express his love and loyalty. And he expressed it some seven times down the length of Prechistenka to Obukhov Lane. He kissed his shoe; near Myortvy Lane, trying to clear the path, he scared some lady with his wild bark so much that she sank down on an advertising pillar; and once or twice he whined to maintain the man's pity.

Some bitch of a stray cat, looking like a Siberian, slipped out of a drain pipe, having caught the scent of the sausage despite the blizzard. Sharik almost lost his mind at the prospect that this rich weirdo who picked up wounded dogs in doorways would pick up this thief too, and he would have to share the processed meat. He snarled and bared his teeth at the cat, and the feline hissed like a hole-riddled water hose, and climbed up the pipe to the second floor. Grrrrrr... arf! Scat! You can't stock up enough from the processing centre for all the freeloaders hanging around on Prechistenka.

The gentleman appreciated the loyalty and right at the fire station, by the window that emitted the pleasant grumble of a French horn, rewarded the dog with a second piece about an ounce smaller.

Silly man. Luring me. Don't worry! I'm not going off on my own. I'll follow you wherever you go.

"*Phweet!* This way!"

Onto Obukhov? By all means. We know this lane very well. *Phweet!*

This way? With pleas— oh, no, sorry. There's a door-man. There's nothing worse than a doorman. Much more dangerous than a street-cleaner. An absolutely hateful breed. More disgusting than cats. A flayer in gold braid.

"Don't be afraid. Go."

"Good evening, Filipp Filippovich."

"Hello, Fyodor."

Now there's a personality for you. My God, what have you found for me, my dog's destiny! What kind of man is this who can bring dogs off the street past doormen into an apartment building run by a council of comrades? Look at that scoundrel – not a word, not a movement! His eyes look disturbed, but in general he is indifferent under his gold-braided cap. As if this is how things should be. That's respect, gentlemen, real respect. Well, and I'm with him and behind him. What, touch me? Here's a bite. I'd love to sink my teeth into your calloused proletarian foot. For all the torment from your brethren. How many times did you poke my face with a broom, eh?

"Come on, come on."

I got it, don't worry. Wherever you go, so do I. You just show me the way, and I'll keep up, despite my miserable side.

Calling down from the stairs: "Were there any letters for me, Fyodor?"

From below, respectfully: "No sir, Filipp Filippovich, there weren't" – then, in an intimate, low tone, adding – "they've moved new tenants into apartment three."

The important canine benefactor turned abruptly on the step, leant over the banister, and asked in horror, "Really?"

His eyes opened wide and his moustache bristled.

The doorman tilted his head, brought his hand to his mouth and confirmed it. "Yes sir, a total of four of them."

"My God! I can just imagine the state of the apartment now. And what did they say?"

"Nothing."

"And Fyodor Pavlovich?"

"He went out for screens and bricks. To make partitions."

"I'll be damned!"

"They'll be moving people into all the apartments, Filipp Filippovich, except yours. There was a meeting; they elected a new council of comrades and sent the old one packing."

"The goings-on. Ai-ai-ai... *Phweet.*"

I'm on my way, hurrying. My side is making itself felt, you see. Allow me to lick your boot.

The doorman's gold braid vanished below. The marble landing was warm from the pipes, we turned one more time and reached the first floor.

Chapter 2

THERE'S ABSOLUTELY NO REASON to learn how to read when you can smell meat a mile away. Nevertheless, if you live in Moscow and you have a modicum of sense in your head, you learn some reading willy-nilly, and without taking any courses. Of the forty thousand Moscow dogs there must only be one total idiot who can't make out the word "sausage" syllable by syllable. Sharik started learning by colour. He had just turned four months when they hung greenish blue signs all over Moscow with the words "MSPO Meat Trade". We repeat, none of that is needed because you can smell meat anyway. And there was some confusion once: going by the toxic blue colour, Sharik, whose nose was masked by the petrol fumes of cars, ran into the Golubizner Brothers' electrical-goods shop on Myasnitskaya Street instead of a butcher shop. There, at the brothers' shop, the dog felt the sting of insulated wire, which is a lot tougher than a coachman's whip. That famous moment should be considered the start of Sharik's education. Back on the pavement, Sharik immediately understood that "blue" doesn't always mean "meat" and, tucking his tail between his hind legs and howling with pain, he recalled that all the butchers' signs started on the left with a gold or reddish squat squiggle that looks like a sled: "M".

Things went more successfully after that. He learnt "A" from "Glavryba", the fish store on the corner of Mokhovaya, and then the "B" (because it was easier to run over from the tail end of the word for fish, "*ryba*", since there always was a policeman standing at the beginning of the word).

Tile squares on the façades of corners in Moscow always and inevitably meant "Cheese". The black tap of a samovar (the letter "Ch") that started the word stood for the former owner Chichkin, mountains of Dutch red cheese, vicious salesmen who hated dogs, sawdust on the floor and the most vile, stinky Backstein cheese.

If someone was playing a concertina – which wasn't much better than 'Celeste Aida' – and it smelt of hotdogs, the first letters on the white signs quite conveniently formed the word "Foul…" which meant: "Foul language not permitted and no tipping." Here brawls cycloned sporadically, people were punched in the face – albeit rarely – while dogs were beaten continually with napkins or boots.

If the windows displayed leathery hanging hams and piles of mandarin oranges, it was a delicatessen. If there were dark bottles with a bad liquid, it was a woof, wow… w…ine store. The former Yeliseyev Brothers' store.

The unknown gentleman, who had lured the dog to the door of his luxurious apartment on the second floor, rang and the dog looked up at the big card, black with gold letters, hanging to the side of the wide door with panes of wavy, rosy glass. He combined the first three letters right away: puh-ar-o – "Pro". But then came a tubby, double-sided bitch of a letter that didn't stand for anything he knew.*

"Could it be proletariat?" wondered Sharik doubtfully. "That can't be." He raised his nose and sniffed the fur coat once again, and thought confidently: "No, there's no smell of the proletariat here. It's a scholarly word, and God only knows what it means."

Behind the rosy glass an unexpected and joyful light came on, casting the black card deeper into shadow. The door opened without a sound and a pretty young woman in a white apron and lace cap appeared before dog and man. The former was enveloped in divine warmth, and the woman's skirt gave off the scent of lily of the valley.

"Now you're talking, this is it," thought the dog.

"Please enter, Mr Sharik," the man invited sarcastically, and Sharik entered reverently, tail wagging.

A great number of objects cluttered the rich entrance. The floor-length mirror that instantly reflected the second bedraggled and scruffy Sharik, the scary antlers up high, the endless fur coats and rubber boots and the opal tulip with electricity on the ceiling – all stuck in his head immediately.

"Where did you pick up this one, Filipp Filippovich?" asked the woman with a smile and helped him remove his heavy coat, lined with dark-brown fox with a bluish tinge. "Lord! What a mangy thing!"

"Nonsense. Where is he mangy?" the gentleman asked severely and gruffly.

Upon removing his fur coat, he appeared in a black suit of English cloth, and a gold chain twinkled happily and subtly across his belly.

"Just wait, stop wriggling, *phweet*... stop twisting, silly. Hmmm... That's not mange... will you stand still, damn you!... Hmmm... Ah! It's a burn. What bastard scalded you? Eh? Stand still, will you!"

"The cook, the criminal. The cook!" The dog spoke with his piteous eyes and whined a bit.

"Zina," ordered the man, "bring him to the examining room and me my coat!"

The woman whistled and clicked her fingers and the dog, after a brief hesitation, followed her. Together, they entered a narrow, dimly lit corridor, passed a lacquered door and came to the end, and then went left and ended up in a dark cubbyhole, which instantly displeased the dog by its evil smell. The darkness clicked and turned into blinding daylight, and it sparkled, lit up, and turned white from all sides.

"Oh, no," the dog howled mentally, "sorry, not for me! I get it! Damn them and their sausage! They've lured me into a dog hospital. They'll force me to eat castor oil and they'll cut up my side with knives, and it hurts too much to touch as it is!"

"Hey, no! Where do you think you're going!" shouted the one called Zina.

The dog twisted away, coiled up, and then hit the door with its healthy side so hard that the whole apartment shuddered. Then he flew back, spun around in place like a top, and knocked over a white bucket that scattered clumps of cotton wool. As he spun, walls flew by, fitted with cupboards of gleaming instruments, and the white apron and distorted female face jumped up.

"Where are you going, you shaggy devil!" Zina shouted desperately. "Damn you!"

"Where's the back stairs?" thought the dog. He reversed and smashed himself against the glass, hoping that it was a second door. A cloud of glass shards flew out with thunder and ringing, a tubby jar with reddish crap jumped out, spilling all over the floor and stinking up the room. The real door swung open.

"Stop! B-bastard!" The man shouted, jumping around in his white coat with only one sleeve on, and grabbed the dog by its legs. "Zina, hold him by the scruff of his neck, the scoundrel!"

"Wow! What a dog!"

The door opened even wider and another person of the male gender in a white coat burst in. Crushing broken glass, he rushed not towards the dog but the cupboard, opened it, and the whole room was filled with a sweet and nauseating odour. Then the person fell onto the dog with his belly, and the dog took pleasure in nipping him above the shoelaces. The person gasped but held on. The nauseating liquid filled the dog's breathing and everything in his head spun, then he couldn't feel his legs and he slid off somewhere sideways, crookedly.

"Thanks, it's over," he thought dreamily, falling right on the sharp pieces of glass, "farewell, Moscow! I'll never see Chichkin and proletarians and Cracow sausages again! I'm going to Heaven for my canine suffering. Fellows, knackers, why did you do me in?"

And then he fell over on his side completely and croaked.

When he was resurrected, his head spun lightly and he had a bit of nausea in his belly, but it was if he had no side; his side was deliciously silent. The dog half-opened his right eye and out of the corner saw that he was tightly bandaged across his sides and belly. "They had their way after all, the sons-of-bitches," he thought woozily, "but cleverly, you have to give them that."

"From Seville to Granada... in the quiet twilight of the nights,"* a distracted falsetto voice sang above him.

The dog was surprised; he opened both eyes fully and saw two steps away from him a man's foot on a white stool. The trouser leg and long underpants were hiked up and the bare yellow shin was smeared with dried blood and iodine.

"Saints alive!" thought the dog. "That must be where I bit him. My work. They'll whip me now!"

"'Serenades abound, swords clash all around!' Why did you bite a doctor, you mutt? Eh? Why did you break the glass? Eh?"

"Ooo-ooo-ooo," the dog whimpered piteously.

"Well, all right, you're conscious, so just lie there, you dummy."

"How did you manage to lure such a nervous dog, Filipp Filippovich?" asked a pleasant male voice, and the knit underpants slid down. Tobacco smoke filled the air, and glass bottles rattled in the cupboard.

"With kindness. It's the only way possible in dealing with a living creature. Terror won't work at all with an animal, at whatever level of development it may be. I've said it before and I say it again and will continue saying it. They're wrong to think that terror will help them. No, no, it won't, whatever its colour: white, red or even brown! Terror paralyses the nervous system completely. Zina! I bought this wastrel a rouble and forty copecks' worth of Cracow sausage. Be so kind as to feed him when he's no longer nauseated."

Broken glass tinkled as it was swept up, and a woman's voice noted flirtatiously: "Cracow sausage! God, you should have gotten him two copecks' worth of scraps at the butcher! I'll eat the Cracow sausage myself."

"Just try! I'll eat you! It's poison for the human stomach. A grown young woman and you're like a baby sticking all kinds of nasty things in your mouth. Don't you dare! I'm warning you, neither Doctor Bormental nor I will bother with you when you get the runs. 'Everyone who says that another is your match…'"

Soft staccato bells jingled throughout the apartment, and in the distance voices sounded frequently in the entrance. The telephone rang. Zina vanished.

Filipp Filippovich tossed his cigarette butt in the bucket, buttoned his coat, smoothed his luxurious moustache in the mirror on the wall and called the dog.

"*Phweet, phweet*… come on, come on, it's fine! Let's go receive."

The dog got up on unsteady legs, swayed and trembled, but quickly got his bearings and followed the fluttering coat-tails of Filipp Filippovich. Once again the dog crossed the narrow corridor, but now he saw that it was brightly lit from above. When the lacquered door opened, he followed Filipp Filippovich into the office, which blinded the dog with its interior. First of all, it was blazing with light: it burned on the plaster ornamented ceiling, it burned on the desk, it burned on the wall and in the cupboard glass. Light poured over a myriad of objects, of which the most amusing was an enormous owl, sitting on a branch on the wall.

"Stay," ordered Filipp Filippovich.

The carved door opposite opened and the bitten man came in, and now in the bright light revealed as a very handsome young fellow with a pointy beard, and handed over a piece of paper, muttering, "The previous…"

He vanished silently, while Filipp Filippovich smoothed the tails of his lab coat and sat behind the huge desk, thereby becoming incredibly important and imposing.

"No, this isn't a hospital, I've landed in some other place," the dog thought in confusion and flopped on the carpet by the heavy leather sofa, "and we'll figure out that owl too."

The door opened softly and someone came in, astonishing the dog enough to make him yap, but very diffidently.

"Quiet! Well, well, well! You're unrecognizable, dear fellow."

The newcomer bowed very respectfully and awkwardly to Filipp Filippovich.

"Hee-hee! You are a magician and sorcerer, professor," he muttered in embarrassment.

"Take off your pants, dear fellow," Filipp Filippovich commanded and stood up.

"Jesus!" thought the dog. "What a fruitcake!"

The fruitcake's head was covered with completely green hair, and at the back it had a rusty tobacco shimmer. Wrinkles spread out on the fruitcake's face, but his complexion was as pink as a baby's. His left leg couldn't bend and he had to drag it along the carpet, but the right one jerked like a toy nutcracker. On the lapel of his magnificent jacket, a precious stone protruded like an eye.

The dog was so interested that his nausea passed.

"Yip, yip," he barked softly.

"Quiet! How are you sleeping, dear fellow?"

"Hee-hee… Are we alone, professor? It's indescribable," the visitor said in embarrassment. "*Parole d'honneur,** I've seen nothing like it for twenty-five years!" The subject touched the button of his trousers. "Can you believe it, Professor? Every night there are herds of naked girls… I am positively delighted. You are a sorcerer!"

"Hmmm," grunted Filipp Filippovich in concern, peering into his guest's pupils.

The latter had finally mastered the buttons and removed his striped trousers. Beneath them were unimaginable underpants. They were cream-coloured, with embroidered black

silk cats, and they smelt of perfume. The dog couldn't resist
the cats and barked, making the subject jump.

"Ai!"

"I'll whip you! Don't be afraid, he doesn't bite."

"I don't bite?" the dog was surprised.

A small envelope, with a picture of a beautiful girl with
loosened tresses, fell out of the trousers pocket onto the
floor. The subject jumped up, bent over, picked it up and
blushed a deep red.

"You'd better watch it," Filipp Filippovich warned grimly,
wagging his finger, "Do be careful not to abuse it!"

'I'm not abu…" the subject muttered in embarrassment, still undressing. "This was just an experiment, dear
Professor."

"Well, and what were the results?" Filipp Filippovich
asked sternly.

The subject waved his arm ecstatically.

"In twenty-five years, I swear to God, Professor, there
was nothing like it! The last time was in 1899 in Paris on
the Rue de la Paix."

"And why have you turned green?"

The visitor's face darkened.

"That damned Zhirkost!* You cannot imagine what those
useless louts fobbed off on me instead of dye. Just look,"
he babbled, his eyes searching for a mirror. "It's terrible!
They should be punched in the face," he added, growing
angrier. "What I am supposed to do now, Professor?" he
asked snivelling.

"Hm… Shave it all off."

"Professor!" the visitor exclaimed piteously, "It will grow
back grey again! Besides which, I won't be able to show my
face at work, I've been out three days now as it is. The car

comes for me and I send it away. Oh, Professor, if you could discover a way of rejuvenating hair as well!"

"Not right away, not right away, dear fellow," muttered Filipp Filippovich.

Bending over, he examined the patient's bare belly with glistening eyes. "Well, it's lovely, everything is perfectly fine… I didn't expect such a fine result, truth to tell… 'Lots of blood and lots of songs!'… Get dressed, dear fellow!"

"'And for the loveliest of all!…' the patient sang the next line in a voice as resonant as a frying pan and, glowing, started dressing. Having brought himself back to order, hopping and exuding perfume, he counted out a wad of white banknotes for Filipp Filippovich and tenderly pressed both of his hands.

"You need not return for two weeks," Filipp Filippovich said, "but I do ask that you be careful."

"Professor!" from beyond the door, in ecstasy, the guest exclaimed. "Do not worry in the least." He giggled sweetly and vanished.

The tinkling bell flew through the apartment, the lacquered door opened, the bitten one entered, handing Filipp Filippovich a piece of paper and announced: "The dates are incorrectly given. Probably 54–55. Heart tones low."

He vanished and was replaced by a rustling lady with a hat at a rakish angle and a sparkling necklace on her flabby and wrinkled neck. Terrible black bags sagged beneath her eyes, but her cheeks were a doll's rouge colour.

She was very agitated.

"Madam! How old are you?" Filipp Filippovich asked very severely.

The lady took flight and even paled beneath the crust of rouge.

"I, Professor... I swear, if you only knew, my drama..."

"How old, Madam?" Filipp Filippovich repeated even more severely.

"Honestly... well, forty-five—"

"Madam!" Filipp Filippovich cried out. "People are waiting! Don't hold me up, please, you are not the only one!"

The lady's bosom heaved mightily.

"I'll tell you alone, as a luminary of science, but I swear, it is so terrible—"

"How old are you?" Filipp Filippovich demanded angrily and squeakily, and his glasses flashed.

"Fifty-one," the lady replied, cowering in fear.

"Take off your pants, Madame," Filipp Filippovich said in relief and indicated a tall white scaffold in the corner.

"I swear, Professor," the lady muttered, undoing some snaps on her belt with trembling fingers, "That Moritz... I am confessing to you, hiding nothing..."

"'From Seville to Granada,'" Filipp Filippovich sang distractedly and stepped on the pedal under the marble sink. Water poured noisily.

"I swear to God!" the lady said, and live spots of colour broke through the artificial ones on her cheeks, "I know that this is my last passion... He's such a scoundrel! Oh, Professor! He's a card shark, all of Moscow knows it. He can't let a single lousy model get by. He's so devilishly young!" The lady mumbled and pulled out a crumpled lacy clump from beneath her rustling skirts.

The dog was completely confused and everything went belly up in his head.

"The hell with you," he thought dimly, resting his head on his paws and falling asleep from the shame, "I won't

22

even try to understand what this is, since I won't get it anyway."

He was awaked by a ringing sound and saw that Filipp Filippovich had tossed some glowing tubes into a basin.

The spotted lady, pressing her hands to her breast, gazed hopefully at Filipp Filippovich. He frowned importantly and, sitting at his desk, made a notation.

"Madame, I will transplant ape ovaries in you," he announced and looked severe.

"Ah, Professor, must it be an ape?"

"Yes," Filipp Filippovich replied inexorably.

"When will the operation take place?" the lady asked in a weak voice, turning pale.

"'From Seville to Granada'... hm... Monday. You will check into the clinic in the morning and my assistant will prepare you."

"Ah, I don't want to be in the clinic. Can't you do it here, Professor?"

"You see, I do surgery here only in extreme situations. It will be very expensive, five thousand."

"I'm willing, Professor!"

The water thundered again, the feathered hat billowed, and then a head as bald as a plate appeared and embraced Filipp Filippovich. The dog dozed, the nausea had passed, and the dog enjoyed the calmed side and warmth, even snored a little and had time for a bit of a pleasant dream: he had torn a whole bunch of feathers from the owl's tail... Then an agitated voice bleated overhead:

"I am a well-known figure, Professor! What do I do now?"

"Gentlemen!" Filipp Filippovich shouted in outrage. "You can't behave this way! You have to control yourself! How old is she?"

"Fourteen, Professor... You realize that the publicity will destroy me. I'm supposed to be sent to London on business any day now."

"I'm not a lawyer, dear fellow... So, wait two years and marry her."

"I'm married, Professor!"

"Ah, gentlemen, gentlemen!"

Doors opened, faces changed, instruments clattered in the cupboard, and Filipp Filippovich worked without stop.

"A vile apartment," the dog thought, "but how good it is here! What the hell did he need me for? Is he really going to let me live? What a weirdo! A single wink from him and he'd get such a fine dog it would take your breath away! Maybe I'm handsome too. It's my good luck! But the owl is garbage. Arrogant."

The dog woke up at last late in the evening, when the bells stopped and just at the instant when the door let in special visitors. There were four at once. All young people, and all dressed very modestly.

"What do these want?" the dog thought with surprise. Filipp Filippovich greeted them with much greater hostility. He stood at his desk and regarded them like a general looking at the enemy. The nostrils of his aquiline nose flared. The arrivals shuffled their feet on the carpet.

"We are here, Professor," said the one with a topknot of about a half foot of thick, curly black hair, "on this matter—"

"Gentlemen, you shouldn't go around without galoshes in this weather," Filipp Filippovich interrupted edifyingly. "First, you will catch cold, and second, you've left tracks on my carpets, and all my carpets are Persian."

The one with the topknot shut up and all four stared in astonishment at Filipp Filippovich. The silence extended to several seconds and it was broken by Filipp Filippovich's fingers drumming on the painted wooden plate on his desk.

"First of all, we're not gentlemen," said the youngest of the four, who had a peachy look.

"First of all," interrupting him as well, Filipp Filippovich asked, "are you a man or a woman?"

The four shut up and gaped once again. This time the first one, with the hair, responded. "What difference does it make, Comrade?" he asked haughtily.

"I'm a woman," admitted the peachy youth in the leather jacket and blushed mightily. After him, one of the other arrivals, a blond man in a tall fur hat, blushed dark red for some reason.

"In that case, you may keep your cap on; but you, gracious sir, I ask to remove your headgear," Filipp Filippovich said imposingly.

"I'm not your 'gracious sir'," the blond youth muttered in embarrassment, removing his hat.

"We have come to you—" the dark-haired one began again.

"First of all, who is this 'we'?"

"We are the new managing board of our building," the dark one said with contained fury. "I am Shvonder, she is Vyazemskaya, he is Comrade Pestrukhin, and Sharovkin. And so we—"

"You're the ones who have been moved into the apartment of Fyodor Pavlovich Sablin?"

"We are," Shvonder replied.

"God! The Kalabukhov house is doomed!" Filipp Filippovich exclaimed in despair and threw his hands up in the air.

"What are you laughing about, Professor?"

"I'm not laughing! I'm in complete despair!" shouted Filipp Filippovich. "What will happen to the central heating now?"

"You are mocking us, Professor Preobrazhensky!"

"What business brings you here? Make it fast, I'm on my way to dinner."

"We, the Building Committee," Shvonder said with hatred, "have come to you after the general meeting of the residents of our building, on the agenda of which was the question of consolidating the apartments."

"Where was this agenda?" screamed Filipp Filippovich. "Make an effort to express your ideas more clearly."

"The question of consolidating—"

"Enough! I understand! You know that by the resolution of 12th August of this year my apartment is exempt from all and any consolidation and resettlement?"

"We know," Shvonder replied, "but the general meeting examined your case and came to the conclusion that in particular and on the whole you occupy an excessive space. Completely excessive. You live alone in seven rooms."

"I live and work alone in seven rooms," replied Filipp Filippovich, "and I would like to have an eighth. I need it as a library."

The foursome froze.

"An eighth! Ho-ho-ho," said the blond man deprived of his headgear, "that's really something!"

"It's indescribable!" explained the youth who turned out to be a girl.

"I have a reception – note that it is also the library – a dining room and my study – that's three. Examining room, four. Operating room, five. My bedroom makes six, and the maids' room is seven. Basically, it's not enough… But that's not important. My apartment is exempt and that's the end of the conversation. May I go to dinner?"

"Sorry," said the fourth, who looked like a sturdy beetle.

"Sorry," Shvonder interrupted, "it is precisely the dining room and examining room that we came to discuss. The general meeting asks you voluntarily, as part of labour discipline, to give up the dining room. No one has dining rooms in Moscow anymore."

"Not even Isadora Duncan!"* the woman cried out resoundingly.

Something happened to Filipp Filippovich, the consequence of which was a gentle reddening of the face, but he did not utter a sound, waiting for what would come next.

"And the examining room too," Shvonder continued. "The examining room can easily be combined with the study."

"Ah-ha," said Filipp Filippovich in a strange voice. "And where am I supposed to partake of meals?"

"In the bedroom," all four chorused.

Filipp Filippovich's crimson colour took on a greyish cast.

"Take food in the bedroom," he said in a slightly stifled voice, "read in the examining room, dress in the reception room, operate in the maid's room, and examine people in the dining room? It's quite possible that Isadora Duncan does just that. Maybe she dines in the study and cuts up rabbits in the bathroom. Perhaps. But I am not Isadora Duncan!" he burst out, and his purple colour turned yellow. "I will eat in the dining room and operate in the operating room! Tell this to the general meeting, and I entreat you humbly to return to your affairs and allow me to take food where all normal people do – that is, in the dining room, and not in the entrance and not in the nursery."

27

"Then, Professor, in view of your stubborn resistance," said agitated Shvonder, "we will file a complaint against you higher up."

"Aha," Filipp Filippovich said, "is that so?" His voice took on a suspiciously polite tone. "I'll ask you to wait a minute."

"That's some guy," thought the dog delightedly. "Just like me. Oh, he's going to nip them now, oh, he will! I don't know how yet, but he'll nip them!... Hit them! Take that long-legged one right above the boot on his knee tendon... Grrrrr."

Filipp Filippovich picked up the telephone receiver with a bang and said this into it: "Please... yes... thank you. Vitaly Alexandrovich, please. Professor Preobrazhensky. Vitaly Alexandrovich? Very glad to find you in. Thank you, I'm fine. Vitaly Alexandrovich, your operation is being cancelled. What? No, cancelled completely, just like all the other operations. Here is why: I am stopping work in Moscow and in Russia in general... Four people just came in to see me, one of them is a woman dressed as a man and two are armed with revolvers, and they terrorized me in my apartment with the goal of taking part of it away—"

"Excuse me, Professor," Shvonder began, his expression changed.

"Sorry... I do not have the opportunity to repeat everything they said, I'm not interested in nonsense. It is enough to say that they proposed I give up my examining room, in other words, making it necessary to operate on you where I have been slaughtering rabbits until now. In such conditions I not only cannot work but I do not have the right to work. Therefore, I am ending my activity, closing up the apartment, and moving to Sochi. I can turn over the keys to Shvonder, let him perform the operations."

The foursome froze. Snow melted on their boots.

"What else can I do?... I'm very unhappy about it myself... What? Oh, no, Vitaly Alexandrovich! Oh no! I will not continue this way. My patience has run out. This is the second time since August. What? Hm... As you wish. But at least... But only on this condition: from whomever, whenever, whatever, but it must be a paper that will keep Shvonder and everyone else from even approaching the door to my apartment. A final paper. Factual. Real. A seal. So that my name is not even mentioned. Of course. I am dead to them. Yes, yes. Please. Who? Aha... Well, that's better. Aha. All right. I'll pass the phone over. Please be so kind," Filipp Filippovich said in a snake-like voice, "someone wants to speak to you."

"Excuse me, Professor," Shvonder said, flaring up and then fading, "you perverted our words."

"I will ask you not to use such expressions."

Shvonder distractedly took the receiver and said, "I'm listening. Yes... chairman of the BuildCom... We were acting in accordance with the rules... the professor is in a completely exceptional situation as it is... We know about his work... we were going to leave an entire five rooms... well, all right... if that's the case... all right..."

Completely red, he hung up and turned.

"He really showed him! What a guy!" the dog thought in delight. "Does he know some special word? You can beat me all you like now, but I'm not ever leaving here!"

Three of them, mouths agape, stared at the humiliated Shvonder.

"This is shameful," he muttered diffidently.

"If we were to have a discussion now," the woman began, excited and with flaming cheeks, "I would prove to Vitaly Alexandrovich..."

"Forgive me, you're not planning to open the discussion this minute, are you?" Filipp Filippovich asked politely.

The woman's eyes burned.

"I understand your irony, Professor, we will be leaving... Only... As chairman of the cultural section of the building—"

"Chair-wo-man," Filipp Filippovich corrected.

"I want to ask you," and here the woman pulled out several bright and snow-sodden magazines from inside her coat, "to buy a few magazines to help the children of France. Half a rouble each."

"No, I won't," Filipp Filippovich replied brusquely, squinting at the magazines.

Total astonishment showed on their faces, and the woman's complexion took on a cranberry hue.

"Why are you refusing?"

"I don't want to."

"Don't you feel sympathy for the children of France?"

"I do."

"Do you begrudge the fifty copecks?"

"No."

"Then why?"

"I don't want to."

A silence ensued.

"You know, Professor," said the girl after a deep sigh, "If you weren't a European luminary and you weren't protected in the most outrageous manner (the blond man tugged at the hem of her jacket, but she waved him off) by people whom, I am certain, we will discover, you should be arrested!"

"For what exactly?" Filipp Filippovich asked with curiosity.

"You hate the proletariat!" the woman said hotly.

"Yes, I don't like the proletariat," Filipp Filippovich agreed sadly and pressed a button. A bell rang somewhere. The door to the hallway opened.

"Zina," Filipp Filippovich shouted. "Serve dinner. Do you mind, gentlemen?"

The foursome silently left the study, silently went through the reception, silently through the entrance, and behind them came the sound of the front door shutting heavily and resoundingly.

The dog stood on his hind legs and performed a kind of prayer dance before Filipp Filippovich.

Chapter 3

THE DISHES, painted with paradisaical flowers and a wide black rim, held thin slices of salmon and marinated eel. On the heavy board was a chunk of sweating cheese, and in a silver bowl, surrounded by snow, was caviar. Among the plates stood several slender shot glasses and three crystal decanters with vodkas of different colours. All these objects resided on a small marble table cosily nestled up against the enormous carved oak sideboard, erupting with bursts of glass and silver light. In the centre of the room stood a table, as heavy as a gravestone, under a white cloth, and on it were two settings, napkins folded into bishops' mitres and three dark bottles.

Zina brought in a covered silver dish with something grumbling inside. The fragrance coming from the dish made the dog's mouth fill with watery saliva instantly. "The Gardens of Semiramide!"* he thought and started banging his tail like a stick on the parquet floor.

"Bring them here!" Filipp Filippovich commanded with the air of a predator. "Doctor Bormental, I tell you, leave the caviar be! If you would like to take some good advice, have the ordinary Russian vodka, not the English."

The handsome bitten one (he was no longer wearing the lab coat but was in a decent black suit) shrugged his broad shoulders, chuckled politely, and poured himself the clear vodka.

"The newly blessed?"* he enquired.

"Bless you, dear fellow," the host replied. "It's spirit alcohol. Darya Petrovna makes excellent vodka herself."

"You know, Filipp Filippovich, everyone says that it's quite decent now. Sixty proof."

"But vodka must be eighty proof, not sixty, first of all," Filipp Filippovich interrupted with a lecture. "And secondly, God only knows what they may have added to it. Can you predict what they could come up with?"

"Anything at all," the bitten one said confidently.

"I am of the same opinion," added Filipp Filippovich and tossed the contents of his glass as a single lump into his throat. "Eh... Mmm... Doctor Bormental, I entreat you: take this thing instantly, and if you say it's not... then I will be your mortal enemy for life. 'From Seville to Granada...'"

With those words, he hooked something resembling a small dark loaf of bread on his palmate silver fork. The bitten one followed his example. Filipp Filippovich's eyes glowed.

"Is this bad?" Filipp Filippovich asked, chewing. "Is it? You tell me, esteemed doctor."

"It's exquisite," the bitten one replied sincerely.

"Of course... Please note, Ivan Arnoldovich, that only the remaining landowners not yet slaughtered by the Bolsheviks use cold hors d'oeuvres or soup as *zakuski* for vodka.* Any even slightly self-respecting person operates with hot *zakuski*. And of the hot *zakuski* of Moscow, this is number one. They used to be prepared marvellously once upon a time at the Slavyansky Bazaar. Here!"

"You're giving the dog food from the table," a woman's voice sounded, "and then you won't be able to lure him out of here with a fresh-baked round loaf."

"It's all right. The poor thing was starved." Filipp Filippovich used his fork to serve the dog the titbit, which was accepted with prestidigitatorial agility, and then tossed the fork with a clatter into the rinse bowl.

Next, steam redolent of crayfish rose from the plates; the dog sat in the shade of the tablecloth with the air of a watchman at a gunpowder warehouse, while Filipp Filippovich tucked the tail of the taut napkin into his collar and preached: "Food, Ivan Arnoldovich, is a tricky thing. One must know how to eat, and just imagine, the majority of people don't know how at all. One needs to know not only what to eat but when and how." (Filipp Filippovich waved his spoon significantly.) "And what to say, yes! If you care about your digestion, here is good advice – do not talk about Bolshevism or medicine while eating. And, God forbid, don't read Soviet newspapers before dinner!"

"Hm… But there are no others."

"So don't read any. You know, I did thirty observations at my clinic. And what do you think? The patients who did not read newspapers felt wonderful. The ones I had read *Pravda* lost weight!"

"Hm?" the bitten one responded with interest, turning pink with soup and wine.

"Moreover, reduced knee reflexes, poor appetite and depression."

"The Devil!…"

"Yes. But what am I doing? I brought up medicine myself. Let's eat instead."

Filipp Filippovich leant back, rang, and Zina appeared in the cherry-wood doorway. The dog was given a pale and fat piece of sturgeon, which he didn't like, and immediately after it a piece of rare roast beef. Gobbling it down, the dog suddenly realized that he was sleepy and couldn't look at any more food. "A strange sensation," he thought, shutting his heavy lids, "my eyes don't want to see any food. And smoking after dinner is stupid."

The dining room filled with unpleasant blue cigar smoke. The dog dozed, head on top of his front paws.

"Saint-Julien is a decent wine," the dog heard in his sleep, "but you can't get it any more."

A soft chorale, dampened by ceilings and carpets, reached them from above and the side.

Filipp Filippovich rang, and Zina entered.

"Zinusha, what does this mean?"

"They're having a general meeting again, Filipp Filippovich," Zina replied.

"Again!" Filipp Filippovich cried bitterly. "Well, that's the beginning of the end! The Kalabukhov house is doomed! I'll have to move, but where, I ask you? It's a slippery slope. First there will be singing every night, then the pipes will freeze in the toilets, then the boiler will burst in the central heating system, and so on. It's curtains for Kalabukhov!"

"Filipp Filippovich is grieving," Zina noted with a smile and carried away a mound of dishes.

"How could I not grieve?" howled Filipp Filippovich. "What a building this was! You must understand!"

"You take too grim a view of things, Filipp Filippovich," countered the handsome bitten one. "They have changed acutely now."

"Dear fellow, you know me! Right? I am a man of facts, a man of observation. I am an enemy of unsubstantiated hypotheses. And that is very well known not only in Russia but in Europe. If I say something, that means it is based on a fact from which I draw my conclusion. And here is a fact for you: the coat rack and galoshes stand in our building."

"Interesting…"

"Galoshes – that's nonsense, happiness does not lie in galoshes," thought the dog, "but he's an outstanding character."

"Let me put it to you – the galoshes stand. I have lived in this building since 1903. And throughout that time until April 1917 there has not been a single incident – and I underline 'not a single' in red pencil! – of even one pair of galoshes disappearing from our lobby downstairs, with the front door never locked. Note that there are twelve apartments here and I have visiting hours. In April 1917, one fine day all the galoshes disappeared, including two pairs belonging to me, three walking sticks, an overcoat and the doorman's samovar. Ever since then the galoshes stand ceased to exist. My dear fellow! I'm not talking about the central heating! I'm not! Let it be. If we're in a social revolution, there shouldn't be heating! Though someday, if I have the free time, I'll study the brain and prove that all this social twaddle is nothing but delirium… So I say: why, when this whole business began, did everyone start walking in dirty galoshes and felt boots on the marble stairs? Why must the galoshes still be locked up and have a soldier posted to keep them from being swiped? Why did they remove the carpeting from the main staircase? Does Karl Marx* forbid carpets on the stairs? Is it written anywhere in Karl Marx that the second entrance of the Kalabukhov house on Prechistenka must be boarded up and people have to go around through the back door? Who needs that? The oppressed Negroes? Or the Portuguese workers? Why can't the proletariat leave its galoshes downstairs instead of dirtying the marble?"

"But it doesn't even have any galoshes, Filipp Filippovich," the bitten one tried to say.

"Noth-ing of the sort!" Filipp Filippovich replied in thunderous tones and poured a glass of wine. "Hm... I don't approve of liqueurs after dinner, they weigh you down and have a deleterious effect on the liver... Nothing of the sort! The proletariat has galoshes, and those galoshes are mine! They are the very same galoshes that disappeared on 13th April 1917. I ask you, who swiped them? I? Impossible! The bourgeois Sablin?" (Filipp Filippovich pointed at the ceiling.) "Ridiculous to contemplate! The sugar-plant owner Polozov?" (Filipp Filippovich pointed to the side.) "Not in any case! It was done by those songsters! Yes! But why can't they take them off when they're on the stairs?" (Filipp Filippovich was turning purple.) "Why the hell did they remove the flowers from the landings? Why does the electricity, which – God help my memory here – went out twice in twenty years, now dim every single month? Doctor Bormental! Statistics are a cruel thing. You, who are familiar with my latest work, know this better than anyone!"

"It's the ruination, Filipp Filippovich!"

"No," Filipp Filippovich countered with complete confidence, "no, it's not. You be the first, dear Ivan Arnoldovich, to refrain from using that word. It's a mirage, smoke, fiction!" Filipp Filippovich spread his stubby fingers, making two shadows resembling tortoises wriggle on the tablecloth. "What is this ruination of yours? An old hag with a crutch?* A witch who smashed out all the window glass and put out all the lamps? She simply doesn't exist. What do you mean by that word?" Filipp Filippovich demanded angrily from the poor cardboard duck hanging upside down near the buffet, and answered for it. "Here's what it is: if I, instead of operating every evening, start singing in chorus in my apartment, ruination will befall me! If I start, forgive me for saying this, start missing the toilet bowl when I piss, and so do Zina and Darya Petrovna, there will be ruination in the toilet. Therefore, ruination is not in the toilets, it's in people's heads! That means, when those baritones shout 'Beat the ruination!' I laugh." (Filipp Filippovich's face contorted so much that the bitten one gaped.) "I swear, it makes me laugh! It means that every one of them should smack himself on the head! And then, when he beats the world revolution, Engels and Nikolai Romanov,* the oppressed Malayans and other such hallucinations out of his head and starts cleaning out the sheds – his actual job – the ruin will vanish on its own. You cannot serve two gods at once! It is impossible simultaneously to sweep the trolley tracks and save some Spanish beggars! No one can manage that, Doctor, and especially not people who are already two hundred years behind the Europeans in development and still can't button their own trousers very effectively!"

Filipp Filippovich had fallen into a rage. His hawk-like nostrils flared. Strengthened by his full dinner, he thundered like an ancient prophet, and his head sparked silver.

His words fell on the sleepy dog like a quiet underground buzz. Sometimes the owl with the stupid yellow eyes flashed in his dreamy visions; then the vile mug of the executioner in the dirty white cap; then Filipp Filippovich's cavalier's moustache, lit by the harsh electricity from the lampshade; then sleepy sleighs creaked and vanished, while the ravaged piece of roast beef cooked in juices in the dog's stomach.

"He could earn money at rallies," the dog dreamt woozily, "a first-class businessman. Of course, he doesn't seem to be short of funds as it is…"

"Police!" shouted Filipp Filippovich. "Police!"

"Glug-glug-glug!" Bubbles burst in the dog's brain.

"Police! That, and only that! It matters not at all whether he has a badge or a red kepi. Put a policeman next to every person and force that policeman to moderate the vocal outbursts of our citizens. You say, ruination! I will tell you, Doctor, that nothing will change for the better in our building, or in any other building, until you quieten those singers! As soon as they stop their concerts, the situation will improve on its own!"

"You are making counter-revolutionary statements, Filipp Filippovich," joked the bitten one. "Pray God no one hears you!"

"Nothing dangerous!" Filipp Filippovich retorted heatedly. "No counter-revolution! By the way, there's another word I absolutely can't stand! There's no way of knowing what's hidden by it! The Devil only knows! So I say: there is nothing counter-revolutionary in my words. There is only common sense and life experience."

Here Filipp Filippovich moved the tail of the shiny, cracked napkin from his collar, crumpled it up and laid it next to the unfinished glass of red wine. The bitten one immediately stood and thanked him: "*Merci.*"

"Just a minute, Doctor!" Filipp Filippovich stopped him and took out his wallet from his pocket. He squinted, counted out white notes and handed them to the bitten one with the words, "Today, you are owed forty roubles, Ivan Arnoldovich. Here you are!"

The man who suffered the dog bite thanked him and, blushing, stuffed the money into his jacket pocket.

"Will you be needing me this evening, Filipp Filippovich?" he enquired.

"No, thank you, dear fellow. We won't be doing anything today. First of all, the rabbit died, and secondly, they're doing *Aida* at the Bolshoi. I haven't heard it in a long time. I love it… Remember the duet?… Tara… ra-rim…"

"How do you find time for everything, Filipp Filippovich?" the doctor asked respectfully.

"He who never hurries always arrives everywhere on time," explained his host. "Of course, if I were to jump around to various meetings and warble like a nightingale all day instead of doing my actual work, I wouldn't have time to go anywhere." Filipp Filippovich's fingers pressed the button on his watch and the heavenly chimes played in his pocket. "Just after eight… I'll get there for the second act… I am a believer in the division of labour. Let them sing at the Bolshoi, and I'll do surgery. That's fine – and no ruination… Now, Ivan Arnoldovich, keep an eye out: as soon as there is a suitable death, straight from the table into a nutrient liquid and bring it to me!"

"Don't worry, Filipp Filippovich, the pathology anatomists have promised me."

"Excellent, and in the meantime we'll observe this street neurasthenic, give him a good wash. Let his side heal."

"He's concerned about me," thought the dog. "A very good man. I know who he is! He is a good wizard, a witch and magician from a canine fairy tale… This can't be just a dream, can it? What if it is?" (The dog shuddered in his sleep.) "I'll wake up and there won't be anything here. No lamp in silks, no warmth, no satiety. Back to the alley, horrible blizzard, icy asphalt, hunger, mean people… The cafeteria, the snow… God, how hard that will be!"

Chapter 4

B UT NONE OF THAT HAPPENED. It was the alley that melted like a bad dream and did not return.

You could see that the ruination was not so terrible! Despite it, twice a day the grey accordions under the window sill filled with heat, and warmth spread in waves throughout the apartment.

It was perfectly clear: the dog had got the top prize ticket in the canine lottery. His eyes now filled with grateful tears addressed to the wise man of Prechistenka at least twice a day. Besides which, all the cheval glass in the living room, in the reception area between the wardrobes reflected the lucky and handsome dog.

"I am handsome. Perhaps an unknown canine prince incognito," pondered the dog, looking at the shaggy coffee-coloured dog with a satisfied mug strolling in the mirrored distance. "It's quite possible that my grandmother had a fling with a Newfoundland. I see that there is a white spot on my face. Where did it come from, you may ask? Filipp Filippovich is a man of great taste and he wouldn't pick up any old stray dog he came across."

In the course of a week, the dog ate as much as he had in the last six hungry weeks on the streets. But that was only in terms of weight. There was no need to talk about the quality of the food at Filipp Filippovich's. Even if you don't count the mountain of scraps Darya Petrovna bought every day at the market for eighteen copecks, it's enough to mention the dinners at 7 p.m. in the dining room, which the dog attended, despite the protests of the graceful Zina. During these dinners, Filipp Filippovich completely attained the calling of divinity. The dog stood on his hind legs and chewed his jacket... the dog learnt Filipp Filippovich's ring – two full-voiced bursts of the master's push – and flew out barking to greet him in the entrance. The master strode in wearing the dark-brown fox, glistening with a million snowflakes, smelling of tangerines, cigars, perfume, lemons, petrol, eau de cologne, cloth, and his voice, like a commanding trumpet, carried throughout the residence:

"You pig, why did you tear apart the owl? Was it bothering you? Was it, I ask you? Why did you break Professor Mechnikov?"*

"He needs to be whipped, Filipp Filippovich, at least once," Zina said in outrage, "or he'll be thoroughly spoilt. Just look what he did to your galoshes!"

"No one should be whipped," Filipp Filippovich said agitatedly, "remember that once and for all! Humans and animals can be influenced only by suggestion! Did you give him meat today?"

"Lord! He's eaten us out of house and home! How can you ask, Filipp Filippovich? I'm amazed that he doesn't burst!"

"Let him eat to his heart's content!... How did the owl bother you, you hooligan?"

"Oooo-ooo," whined the toadying dog, crawling on his belly, legs twisted out.

Then he was dragged by the scruff of his neck through the reception to the study with great hue and cry. The dog howled, snapped, clawed at the rug and rode on his backside, like in the circus.

In the middle of the study on the rug lay the glass-eyed owl, its torn belly spilling red rags smelling of camphor. A shattered portrait's smithereens were scattered on the desk.

"I left it like this on purpose so that you could enjoy the sight," an upset Zina reported. "He jumped up on the desk, what a scoundrel! And grabbed the owl by the tail, snap! He tore it up before I caught my breath! Rub his nose in the owl, Filipp Filippovich, so he knows not to ruin things!"

And the howling began. They dragged the dog, glued to the rug, to rub his nose in the owl, while the dog wept bitter tears and thought, "Beat me, just don't chase me from the apartment."

"Send the owl to the taxidermist today. Besides that, here is eight roubles plus fifteen copecks for the tram, go to Muir's* and buy him a good collar with a chain."

The next day they put a wide, shiny collar on the dog. At first, when he looked in the mirror, he was very upset, tucked in his tail and went to the bathroom, wondering how to tear it off against a trunk or a box. But very quickly the dog realized that he was a fool. Zina took him for a walk on the chain. On Obukhov Lane the dog walked like a prisoner, burning with shame, but having walked along Prechistenka to the Church of Christ the Saviour, he realized full well what a collar means in life. Wild envy burned in the eyes of every dog they encountered, and near Myortvy Lane some long-limbed stray with a bobbed tail barked and cursed him as aristocratic scum and a suck-up. When they crossed the trolley tracks, the policeman regarded his collar with pleasure and respect, and when they returned, the most amazing thing in his life occurred: Fyodor the doorman personally unlocked the front door and let in Sharik, saying to Zina: "What a shaggy dog Filipp Filippovich has! And astonishingly fat."

"And how! He eats for six!" explained Zina, made rosy and beautiful by the frost.

"A collar is like a briefcase," thought the dog wittily and, wagging his behind, sashayed up to the second floor like an aristocrat.

Now appreciating the collar's value, the dog made his first visit to the main department of paradise, from which he had been categorically banned until now, to wit – the kingdom of the cook, Darya Petrovna. The entire apartment wasn't worth two bits of Darya's kingdom. Every day, flames sparked and roared in the stove, black on top and tiled. The stove crackled. Darya Petrovna's face burned with eternally fiery torment and unquenched passion in the crimson columns. It shone and glistened with fat. Twenty-two artificial diamonds glowed in her fashionably done light hair, combed over her ears and caught in a bun at the nape. Golden pots hung from hooks on the walls, the entire kitchen was a racket of smells, gurgling and hissing in closed vessels…

"Out!" shrieked Darya Petrovna. "Out, you homeless pickpocket! You're the last thing I need in here! I'll take the poker to you—"

"Now, now… Why are you barking at me?" the dog squinted sweetly. "I'm no pickpocket! Can't you see my collar?" He pushed at the door with his side, poking his nose through it.

Sharik the dog had some secret in conquering people's hearts. Two days later he was lying next to the coal basket and watching Darya Petrovna work. She used a sharp narrow knife to chop off the heads and feet of helpless grouse and then like a furious executioner she tore flesh from the bones, pulled entrails out of the hens and twirled something in the meat grinder. At the same time, Sharik tore at a grouse head. Darya Petrovna pulled out pieces of soaked bread from a bowl of milk, mixed them with the ground meat on a board, poured cream over it all, salted it and shaped patties on the same board. The burner roared as if there was a house fire, and inside the skillet things burbled, bubbled and skittered. The damper leapt up with a clang revealing a horrible hell. Spurting, gushing...

In the evening, the stone jaws went dim, and the dark and important Prechistenka night with its lone star showed in the kitchen window above the white half-curtain. In the kitchen, the floor was damp, the pots glowed mysteriously and dully, and a fireman's cap lay on the table. Sharik lay on the warm stove like a lion on the gates and, one ear cocked in curiosity, watched the black-moustachioed and excited man wearing a broad leather belt behind the half-shut door to Zina and Darya Petrovna's room embrace Darya Petrovna. Her face burned with torment and passion, all of it except her cadaverous powdered nose. A crack of light lay on a picture of the black-moustachioed man, and an Easter rose hung down from it.

"You're as persistent as a demon," Darya Petrovna muttered in the semi-darkness. "Stop it. Zina will be back any minute. Really, did you get the rejuvenation treatment too?"

"We don't need it," the man with the black moustache replied in a husky voice, barely able to control himself. "You are so fiery..."

In the evenings, the Prechistenka star was hidden behind heavy drapes, and if there was no performance of *Aida* at the Bolshoi and there was no meeting of the All-Russian

Surgical Society, the god settled into an armchair. There were no lights on the ceiling, and only a single green lamp burned on the desk. Sharik lay on the carpet in the shadows and stared at the horrible business. Human brains lay in a disgustingly toxic and murky liquid in glass jars. The god's hands, bare to the elbow, were covered in reddish rubber gloves, and his slippery dull fingers rummaged in the grooves. Sometimes the god armed himself with a small glinting knife and quietly cut the firm yellow brains.

"To the sacred banks of the Nile,"* sang the god softly, biting his lips and recalling the golden interior of the Bolshoi Theatre.

The pipes were heated to the highest point at that hour. Their warmth rose to the ceiling, spreading from there throughout the room, and in the dog's fur the last flea, as yet not combed out by Filipp Filippovich but already doomed, grew animated. And then the front door shut in the distance.

"Zinka's off to the cinema," thought the dog. "And when she returns, we'll have supper. I think there will be veal cutlets for supper."

On that terrible day, in the morning, Sharik was pricked by a premonition. As a result he suddenly grew morose and ate breakfast – half a cup of oatmeal and yesterday's lamb bone – without any appetite. He moped to the reception and howled lightly at his own reflection. But after Zina took him for a walk on the boulevard, the day went normally. There were no office hours today, because, as you know, there are no office hours on Tuesdays, and the god sat in the study, some heavy books with bright pictures spread on his desk. They waited for lunch. The dog perked up at the thought that the third dish today, as he had definitely learnt in the kitchen, would be turkey. Walking down the corridor, the dog heard the telephone ring unpleasantly and unexpectedly in Filipp Filippovich's study. Filipp Filippovich answered, listened and suddenly grew agitated.

"Excellent," said his voice, "bring him right away, immediately!"

He moved about, rang, and told Zina when she came in to serve lunch quickly. Lunch! Lunch! Lunch! Dishes clattered in the dining room. Zina started rushing about; Darya Petrovna could be heard grumbling in the kitchen that the turkey wasn't done.

The dog grew worried again.

"I don't like a hubbub in the apartment," he thought. No sooner had he thought it than the hubbub took on an even more unpleasant character. Primarily due to the appearance of Doctor Bormental, whom he had once bitten. He brought a bad-smelling suitcase and, without even taking off his coat, rushed off with it down the corridor to the examining room. Filipp Filippovich dropped his unfinished cup of coffee, which never happened, and ran to meet Bormental, which never happened with him either.

"When did he die?" he shouted.

"Three hours ago," Bormental replied, opening the suitcase without removing his snow-covered hat.

"Who died?" thought the dog grumpily and unhappily, getting underfoot. "I can't stand it when people bustle around."

"Get out of the way! Hurry, hurry, hurry!" shouted Filipp Filippovich in all directions and rang all the bells, as it seemed to the dog.

Zina ran in.

"Zina! Put Darya Petrovna on the phone, to write down all calls, let no one come! I need you. Doctor Bormental, I implore you, hurry, hurry!"

"I don't like this, I don't," the dog frowned in offence and wandered around the apartment, while all the bustle was concentrated in the examining room. Zina appeared suddenly in a white coat resembling a shroud and ran back and forth between the examining room and the kitchen.

"Should I get some grub? The hell with them," decided the dog and got a sudden surprise.

"Don't give Sharik anything!" thundered the command from the examining room.

"Like I can keep an eye on him!"

"Lock him up!"

Sharik was lured and locked in the bathroom.

"Rudeness," thought Sharik, sitting in the dim bathroom, "utter stupidity…"

He spent almost quarter of an hour in the bathroom in a strange mood – sometimes angry, sometimes deeply depressed. Everything was dreary and unclear… "Fine, you'll have yourself galoshes tomorrow, my esteemed Filipp Filippovich," he thought. "You've already had to buy two pairs, now you'll buy another. Teach you to lock up dogs."

But suddenly his furious thought was interrupted. Unexpectedly and clearly he recalled a piece of his earliest youth, the sunny huge expanse of the courtyard near the Preobrazhenskaya Gate, the shards of sunshine in bottles, the broken brick, the free stray dogs…

"No, no way can I leave here to be free, why lie," said the dog drearily, breathing through his nose, "I'm used to it. I'm a gentleman's dog, an intelligent creature; I've tasted a better life. And what is freedom anyway? Just smoke, a mirage, a fiction... The delirium of those miserable democrats..."

Then the dimness in the bathroom became terrible; he howled, threw himself against the door, began scratching at it.

"Ooo-ooo-ooo!" The sound travelled through the apartment as if in a barrel.

"I'll tear up the owl again!" the dog thought wildly, but impotently. Then he weakened, lay still, and when he stood up again, his hackles rose: for some reason he imagined the disgusting eyes of a wolf in the bath...

At the peak of his torment, the door opened. The dog came out, shook himself, and gloomily headed for the kitchen, but Zina firmly led him by the collar to the examining room. A chill shot below the dog's heart.

"What do they need me for?" he thought suspiciously. "My side has healed. I don't understand."

And his paws slid over the slippery parquet floor, and that's how he was delivered to the examining room. He was struck right away by the unusual lighting. The white globe on the ceiling glowed so much that it hurt his eyes. In the white radiance stood a priest, softly singing about the sacred banks of the Nile. Only a vague scent let him recognize Filipp Filippovich. His trimmed grey hair was hidden under a white cap that resembled a patriarch's skullcap. The priest was all in white, and over the white, like a scapular, was a narrow rubber apron. His hands were in black gloves.

The bitten one was also wearing a skullcap. The long table was unfolded, and a small square one on a shiny leg had been moved next to it.

Here the dog began to hate the bitten one more than anything, and mostly because of his eyes today. Usually bold and direct, now they ran in all directions away from the dog's eyes. They were tense, false, and in their depths was hidden a bad, nasty deed, if not an entire crime. The dog gave him a heavy, troubled look and went into the corner.

"The collar, Zina," Filipp Filippovich said softly. "Just don't excite him."

Zina's eyes instantly became just as vile as the bitten one's. She came over to the dog and petted him with blatant falseness. He gave her a sad and scornful look.

"Well, there's three of you. You'll get me if you want. But you're ashamed... If I only knew what you're going to do with me."

Zina undid his collar, the dog shook his head and snorted. The bitten one arose before him with a vile, dizzying odour coming from him.

"Pfui, disgusting... Why do I feel so dizzy and afraid?" thought the dog and backed away from the bitten one.

"Hurry, Doctor," Filipp Filippovich said impatiently.

There was a sharp, sweet smell in the air. The bitten one, never taking his wary, lousy eyes from the dog, took his right hand from behind his back and quickly poked the dog's nose with a wad of damp cotton. Sharik was stunned, his head spun lightly, but he managed to back away. The bitten one leapt after him and suddenly plastered his face with the cotton. His breathing was blocked, but the dog managed to struggle free once more. "Villain," flashed through his mind. "What for?" They plastered his nose again. Suddenly, in the middle of the examining room a lake appeared with very cheery spectral pink dogs in rowing boats on it. His legs lost their bones and bent.

"On the table!" Filipp Filippovich's words crashed somewhere in a merry voice and dissolved in orange streams. The horror vanished, replaced by joy, and for about two seconds the fading dog loved the bitten one. Then the whole world turned upside down and he still felt a cold but pleasant hand under his belly. Then – nothing.

The dog Sharik lay splayed on the narrow operating table, and his head beat helplessly on the white oilcloth pillow. His stomach was shaved and now Doctor Bormental, panting and hurrying, shaved Sharik's head with a machine, digging into the fur. Filipp Filippovich, leaning his hands on the edge of the table, watched the procedure with his eyes as shiny as the gold frames of his glasses, and spoke in agitation:

"Ivan Arnoldovich, the most important moment is when I enter the *sella turcica.** Instantly, I implore you, hand me the appendage and sew immediately! If it starts haemorrhaging there, we'll lose time and we'll lose the dog. Actually, there's no chance for him anyway." He paused, squinting one eye, and glanced, mockingly it seemed, into the half-open sleeping eye of the dog, adding, "You know, I'm sorry for him. Just imagine, I'd grown used to him."

He waved his hands as he spoke, as if blessing the miserable dog Sharik before his difficult exploit. He was trying to keep any dust from landing on the black rubber.

The whitish skin of the dog glimmered beneath the shaved fur. Bormental tossed away the machine and armed himself with a razor. He soaped up the small, helpless head and started shaving. There was a strong crackling coming from the blade, and blood appeared in spots. Having finished shaving the head, the bitten one wiped it with a wet benzene rag, then stretched out the dog's naked belly, blew air out of his lips and said, "Ready."

Zina turned on the water in the sink and Bormental rushed to wash his hands. Zina poured alcohol over them from a vial.

"May I leave, Filipp Filippovich?" she asked, with a fearful look at the dog's shaved head.

"You may."

Zina vanished. Bormental bustled further. He tucked light gauze napkins all around Sharik's head, and then a never-seen bald canine skull and a strange bearded muzzle appeared on the pillow.

The priest moved. He straightened, looked at the dog's head, and said, "Well, bless us, Lord. Scalpel."

Bormental pulled out a small tubby knife from the sparkling pile on the little table and handed it to the priest. Then he donned black gloves just like the priest's.

"Is he asleep?" Filipp Filippovich asked.

"Fast asleep."

Filipp Filippovich's teeth clenched, his little eyes took on a sharp, spiky gleam and, raising up the scalpel, he drew a precise and long cut along Sharik's belly. The skin separated instantly, and blood spurted out in different directions. Bormental pounced like a predator, pressing on Sharik's wound with clumps of gauze, and then used small tweezers, like sugar tongs, to clamp its edges and it dried. Sweat broke out in bubbles on Bormental's brow.

Filipp Filippovich sliced a second time, and they both started tearing at Sharik's body with hooks, scissors and some sort of staples. Pink and yellow tissue, weeping with bloody dew, flew out. Filipp Filippovich twirled his knife in the body and then shouted, "Scissors!"

The instrument flashed in the bitten one's hands as if he were a magician. Filipp Filippovich dug deep and in a few turns tore out Sharik's testicles with some dangling bits from his body. Bormental, completely wet with effort and excitement, rushed to a glass jar and removed other, wet and drooping testicles. Short damp strings leapt and twisted in the hands of the professor and assistant. Crooked needles clicked in the clamps, and the testicles were sewn in place of Sharik's. The priest fell back from the wound, poked it with a clump of gauze and ordered, "Sew up the skin instantly, Doctor!"

Then he looked over at the round white clock.

"We took fourteen minutes," Bormental said through clenched teeth, digging the crooked needle into the flabby skin.

Then both men grew more agitated, like murderers who were in a hurry.

"Scalpel!" shouted Filipp Filippovich.

The scalpel jumped into his hand as if by itself, after which Filipp Filippovich's face grew terrible. He bared his porcelain and gold crowns and in one stroke drew a bloody crown on Sharik's brow. They flipped over the skin with shorn hair like a scalp. They revealed the skull. Filipp Filippovich shouted, "Trepan!"

Bormental handed him the gleaming hand drill. Biting his lips, Filipp Filippovich began jabbing the instrument into the skull and drilling little holes a centimetre apart, so that they went all around the skull. He spent no more than five seconds per hole. Then using an unusual saw, sticking its tail into the first hole, he started sawing the way ladies' sewing kits are made. The skull buzzed and shook softly. In about three minutes they removed the top of Sharik's skull.

That revealed the dome of Sharik's brain, grey with bluish veins and reddish spots. Filipp Filippovich dug into the membranes with the scissors and opened them up. At one point, a thin fountain of blood gushed out, almost hitting the professor in the eye, spotting his cap. Bormental leapt like a tiger with artery forceps to staunch it and succeeded. Sweat slid in torrents from Bormental and his face turned meaty and multicoloured. His eyes raced from Filipp Filippovich's hands to the plate on the table. Filipp Filippovich had become positively terrifying. Hissing sounds came from his nose and his teeth were bared to the gums. He tore off the membrane from the brain and went deep inside, moving the hemispheres of the brain out of the opened bowl. At that moment Bormental went pale, grabbed Sharik's chest with one hand, and said hoarsely, "His pulse is falling rapidly."

Filipp Filippovich gave him a wild look, muttered something and dug in deeper. Bormental broke a glass ampoule with a crunch, sucked it into a hypodermic needle and treacherously injected Sharik somewhere near his heart.

"I'm headed for the *sella turcica*!" roared Filipp Filippovich and with his bloody, slippery gloves removed Sharik's yellow-grey brain from his head. For an instant he squinted at Sharik's muzzle, and Bormental immediately broke a second ampoule with yellow liquid and sucked it into a long hypodermic.

"Into the heart?" he asked meekly.

"Why are you still asking?" the professor roared angrily. "He's died on you five times by now. Inject! It's unthinkable!" His face had come to resemble an inspired highway robber.

The doctor took a swing and inserted the needle into the dog's heart.

"He's alive, just barely," he whispered meekly.

"There no time to discuss whether he's alive or not," fumed the terrible Filipp Filippovich, "I'm in the *sella*. He'll die anyway... Oh, damn... 'To the sacred banks...' Give me the appendage!"

Bormental handed him a jar in which a white lump dangled on a thread in liquid. "He has no equals in Europe, I swear," thought Bormental. With one hand, Filipp Filippovich pulled out the dangling lump, and with the other, using scissors, cut out a similar lump deep between the splayed hemispheres. He tossed Sharik's lump onto the plate and put the new one into the brain along with the thread and with his short fingers, which had miraculously become slender and flexible, managed to wrap it into place with the amber thread. After that he tossed out some clamps and forceps from Sharik's head, tucked the brain back into the brain pan, leant back and asked more calmly, "Dead, of course?"

"Thready pulse," replied Bormental.

"More adrenalin!"

The professor tossed the membrane over the brain, laid the sawn-off top neatly in place, moved the scalp back, and roared, "Sew!"

Bormental sewed up the head in about five minutes, breaking three needles.

And now on the pillow, a background coloured by blood, appeared Sharik's lifeless, dimmed muzzle with a ring wound around his head. Here Filipp Filippovich leant back completely, like a sated vampire, tore off one glove, shaking out a cloud of sweaty powder, tore a hole in the other, threw it on the floor and called, using the button on the wall. Zina appeared in the doorway, head averted, so as not to see Sharik and the blood.

The priest removed the bloody skullcap with chalky hands and shouted, "Get me a cigarette right now, Zina. All fresh linens and a bath!"

He rested his chin on the edge of the table, opened the dog's right eye with two fingers, peered into the clearly dying eye and said, "There, damn it! He didn't die! Well, he will anyway. Ah, Doctor Bormental, I'm sorry about the dog! He was friendly, albeit wily."

Chapter 5

THE NOTEBOOK of Ivan Arnoldovich Bormental. A thin notebook the size of typing paper. Filled in Bormental's hand. The writing in the first two pages is neat, organized and clear; later, it becomes scrawled, agitated, with many blots.

22 December 1924. Monday.

CASE HISTORY

Laboratory dog approximately two years old. Male. Breed – mutt. Name – Sharik. Fur thin, in clumps, greyish brown with spots, tail the colour of baked milk. Traces of fully healed burn on left side. Nutrition before coming to the professor was poor; after a week's stay, very fat. Weight 8 kg (*exclamation mark*).

Heart, lungs, stomach, temperature within norm.

23 December. At 8.30 p.m. the first such operation in Europe developed by Professor Preobrazhensky was performed: under chloroform, Sharik's testicles were removed and replaced with a man's testicles with appendages and spermatic cords, taken from a 28-yr-old man who died 4 hours and 4 minutes before the operation and kept in sterile physiological liquid developed by Prof. Preobrazhensky.

Immediately thereafter, an appendage of the brain, the pituitary gland, was removed after trepanning the skull and replaced by a human one from the aforementioned man.

Introduced 8 cc of chloroform, 1 syringe of camphor, 2 syringes of adrenalin into the heart.

Reasons for the operation: an experiment by Preobrazhensky to combine transplantation of the pituitary gland and testicles to determine whether the pituitary gland is transplantable and, in the future, its influence on rejuvenation of humans.

Operation was performed by Prof. F.F. Preobrazhensky.

Assisted by Dr I.A. Bormental.

The night after the operation: threatening repeated drops in pulse. Expectation of fatal outcome. Huge doses of camphor per Preobrazhensky.

24 December. Morning – improvement. Respiratory rate doubled, temperature 42. Camphor and caffeine subcutaneously.

25 December. Deterioration of condition again. Pulse barely detected, cooling of extremities, no response in pupils. Adrenalin in the heart and camphor per Preobrazhensky, saline intravenously.

26 December. Some improvement. Pulse 180, respiration 92, temperature 41. Camphor, nutrition via enemas.

27 December. Pulse 152, breathing 50, temperature 39.8. Pupils respond. Camphor subcutaneously.

28 December. Significant improvement. At noon, a sudden drenching sweat. Temperature – 37.0. Surgical wounds in previous condition. Re-bandaging. Appetite appeared. Liquid diet.

29 December. Sudden discovery of fur falling out on forehead and sides of body. Brought in for consultation: professor of Dermatology Faculty Vasily Vasilyevich Bundarev and the director of the Moscow Model Veterinary Institute. They consider the incident never described in the literature. Diagnosis remains unestablished. Temperature normal.

(Written in pencil:)

Tonight first bark (8.15). Noteworthy sharp change in timbre and tone (lower). Bark, instead of word "bow-wow", in syllable "a-o". In coloration, faintly resembles groaning.

30 December. Falling-out of fur has taken on the character of general balding. Weighing revealed unexpected result – weight is 30 kilos due to bone growth (lengthening). Dog still lying as before.

31 December. Colossal appetite.

(A splotch in the notebook. After the ink blot, in hasty scrawl:)

At 12.12 the dog clearly barked the word: "A-b-yr"!!

(There is a break in the notebook and then, apparently by mistake caused by agitation, it says):

1 December.

(Crossed out and corrected:)

1 January 1925. Photographed in the morning. Clearly barks "Abyr", repeating the word loudly and somehow joyfully. At 3 o'clock in the afternoon (*in capital letters*) he laughed, causing the maid Zina to faint.

In the evening pronounced the word "Abyr-valg", "Abyr!" eight times in a row.

(In crooked letters written in pencil:)

The professor deciphered the word "Abyr-valg", it means "Glavryba", the fish store!!! Something monstr—

2 January. Photographed while smiling with magnesium flash.

Got out of bed and confidently stood for half an hour on his hind legs. Almost my height.

(A sheet slipped into the notebook:)

Russian science nearly suffered a tremendous loss.

CASE HISTORY ON PROFESSOR F.F. PREOBRAZHENSKY

At 1.13, Professor Preobrazhensky fell into a deep faint. Falling, he struck his head on a chair leg. Tincture of valerian.

In my presence and Zina's, the dog (if he can be called a dog, that is) rudely cursed Professor Preobrazhensky's mother.

(Break in notes.)

6 January (alternating pencil and violet ink).
   Today, after his tail fell off, he said completely clearly "beer hall". Using the phonograph recorder. What the hell is this!!

I am at a loss!

No more office hours. Starting at 5 p.m. coming from the examining room, where this creature strolls about, clear vulgar cursing and the words "another pair".

7 January. He says many words: "coachman", "no room", "evening gazette", "the best present for children", and all the swear words that exist in the Russian lexicon.
   He looks strange. Fur remains only on the head, chin and chest. The rest is bald with flabby skin. In the area of genitals, a man is forming. The skull has enlarged significantly, the forehead sloping and low.

I swear to God I will go mad.

Filipp Filippovich is still feeling poorly. I do most of the observations (phonograph, photographs).

Rumours are spreading throughout the city.

The consequences are incalculable. Today the whole street was full of wastrels and old women. The gawkers are still standing under our windows. The morning papers had an amazing report: "Rumours of a Martian in Obukhov Lane are baseless. They are being spread by merchants on Sukharevka and they will be severely punished." What Martian, damn it? It's a nightmare!!

It's even better in the *Evening Gazette* – they wrote that an infant was born that plays the violin. There's a drawing of the violin and my photograph and the caption: "Prof. Preobrazhensky, who performed the Caesarean on the mother." This is… indescribable… His new word: "policeman".

Turns out, Darya Petrovna was in love with me and stole my photo from F.F.'s album. After I chased out the reporters, one sneaked into the kitchen, and so on.

What goes on during office hours! There were 82 calls today. The telephone is unplugged. Childless ladies have gone mad and are coming…

The BuildCom headed by Shvonder. Why they came, they don't know themselves.

8 January. Late this evening, we came up with the diagnosis. F.F., like a true scientist, admitted his mistake – replacing the pituitary gland does not yield rejuvenation but complete humanization (*underlined three times*). This does not in any way lessen his astonishing, amazing discovery.

That one walked around the apartment today for the first time. He laughed in the corridor, looking at the electric light. Then, accompanied by Filipp Filippovich and myself, he continued into the study. He is steady on his hind (*crossed out*) legs and looks like a small and poorly built man.

He laughed in the study. His smile is unpleasant and somehow artificial. Then he scratched his head, looked around, and I took down a new, clearly enunciated world: "bourgeois". He swore. His swearing is methodical, ceaseless and, apparently, completely meaningless. It bears a rather phonographic character: as if this creature had heard swear words somewhere, automatically and unconsciously recorded them in his brain, and was now bringing them up in packets. But, of course, I'm not a psychiatrist, damn it!

The cursing has a surprisingly depressive effect on Filipp Filippovich. There are moments when he escapes his restrained and cold observation of new phenomena and seems to lose his patience. Thus, during the cursing, he suddenly shouted nervously: "Down!"

This had no effect.

After the walk in the study, with our joint efforts Sharik was forced back into the examining room.

After that Filipp Filippovich and I had a conference. This is the first time, I must admit, that I have seen this confident and astonishingly intelligent man at a loss. Humming as usual, he asked, "What will we do now?" And he replied himself, literally this way: "MoscTailor, yes... 'From Seville to Granada.' MoscTailor, dear doctor." I understood nothing. He explained, "I am asking you, Ivan Arnoldovich, to buy him linens, trousers and a jacket."

9 January. His vocabulary is enriched every five minutes (on average) by a new word and, since this morning, phrases. It seems that they were frozen in his consciousness and are thawing and coming out. The new words remain in use. Since yesterday, I have recorded on the phonograph: "don't push", "beat him", "scoundrel", "get off the step", "I'll show you", "American acclaim" and "primus".

10 January. The dressing took place. He permitted the undershirt readily, even laughing merrily. He refused the underpants, expressing his protest with hoarse cries: "Get in line, you sons of bitches, get in line!" He was dressed. The socks are too big.

(Schematic drawings in the notebooks, apparently depicting the transformation of a dog's leg into a human one.)

The back half of the foot skeleton (Tarsus) lengthens. The toes extend.
   Claws.
   Repeated systematic training on visiting toilet.
   The maid is completely depressed.
   But the creature's comprehension must be noted. Things are moving in the right direction.

11 January. He's completely accepted trousers. Said a long, cheerful phrase, touching Filipp Filippovich's trousers: "Gimme a smoke, your pants are a joke."

The fur on his head is weak and silky. Easily confused with hair. But the spots remain on his temples. Today the last of the fuzz wore off his ears. Colossal appetite. Enjoyed the herring.

At five o'clock an event: for the first time, the words spoken by the creature were not at a remove from surrounding events but were a reaction to them. To wit, when the professor ordered, "Don't throw bones on the floor," he responded unexpectedly, "Shove off, pal!"

F.F. was astonished, then collected himself and said, "If you ever dare to swear at me or the doctor, you will be punished."

I photographed Sharik at that moment. I swear that he understood the professor's words. A sullen shadow fell over his face. He looked up in irritation from beneath his brows, but he quietened down.

Hurrah, he understands!

12 January. Putting hands in pockets. Training him not to curse.

He whistled 'Oh, Little Apple'. *

Holds up his end of a conversation.

I can't refrain from several hypotheses: the hell with rejuvenation for now! The other is immeasurably more important: Professor Preobrazhensky's amazing experiment has revealed one of the secrets of the human brain! Now the mysterious function of the pituitary gland – the brain's appendage – has been clarified! It determines the human image! Its hormones can be called the most important in the organism – the hormones of image! A new area in science is opened: without using Faust's retort a homunculus is created! The surgeon's scalpel brought a new human unit into life! Professor Preobrazhensky, you are a creator!!!

(Ink blot)

But, I digress… And so, he holds up his end of a conversation. As I see it, this is the situation: the transplanted pituitary gland opened the speech centre in the dog's brain, and the words gushed in torrents. I think that we are seeing a revived, developed brain and not a newly created brain. O, marvellous confirmation of the theory of evolution! O, the great chain from dog to Mendeleyev the chemist!*

Here is another of my hypotheses: Sharik's brain in the canine period of his life accumulated a ton of concepts. All the words that he used first were street words which he had heard and kept in his brain. Now, walking down the street, I look at dogs with hidden horror. God only knows what's in their brains!

Sharik can read. Read!!! (*Three exclamation marks.*) I was the one to guess it! From Glavryba! He read it backwards from the end! And I even know where the solution to this puzzle lies: in the decussation of the dog's optic nerves!

What's going on in Moscow is beyond human comprehension! Seven Sukharevsky merchants have been imprisoned for spreading rumours about the doomsday brought on by the Bolsheviks. Darya Petrovna said and even named the date: 28 November 1925, the day of St Stefan the Martyr, the Earth will hit the heavenly axis!! Some swindlers are already giving lectures. We've created such a hullabaloo with that pituitary that I just want to flee the apartment! I've moved into Preobrazhensky's at his request and I sleep in the reception room with Sharik. The examining room has been turned into the reception. Shvonder was right. The BuildCom is gloating. There are no panes left in any of the cupboards, because he was jumping. We barely taught him to stop.

Something terrible is happening to Filipp. When I told him about my hypotheses and my hope to develop Sharik into a psychologically elevated individual, he snorted and replied, "Really?" His tone was vicious. Could I be mistaken? The old man has come up with something. While I struggle with the case history, he pores over the case history of the man whose pituitary gland we removed.

(Inserted sheet in the notebook.)

Klim Grigoryevich Chugunkin, 25. Bachelor. No party membership, a sympathizer. Tried three times and acquitted: the first time because of lack of evidence; the second, his origins saved him; and the third, he got a suspended sentence of 15 years' hard labour. Theft. Profession: playing the balalaika in taverns. Short, poorly built. Swollen liver (alcohol). Cause of death – stabbed in the heart at the Stop Signal Bar near the Preobrazhenskaya Gate.

The old man sits with Klim's chart without cease. I don't understand the point. He muttered something about not having had the sense to examine Chugunkin's entire body at the morgue. I just don't understand! Does it matter whose pituitary gland it is?

17 January. I haven't made notes in several days: had influenza. Over that time, the image has formed completely:

a) completely human in body;
b) weight around 100 lbs;
c) short stature;
d) small head;
e) has started smoking:
f) eats human food;
g) dresses independently;
h) converses fluently.

That's some pituitary! (*Blot.*)

Herewith I end the medical history. Before us is a new organism, and it must be observed from the beginning.

Attachments: transcripts of speech, phonograph recordings, photographic pictures.

Signed: assistant to Professor F.F. Preobrazhensky,

Doctor Bormental

Chapter 6

I T WAS A WINTER EVENING. Late January. Before dinner, before office hours. A sheet of white paper hung on a hook by the door to the reception room, on which was written in Filipp Filippovich's hand:

I forbid eating sunflower seeds in the apartment.
F. Preobrazhensky

And in blue pencil with letters as large as pastries, in Bormental's hand:

Playing musical instruments between the hours of 5 p.m. and 7 a.m. is forbidden.

Then in Zina's hand:

When you get back, tell Filipp Filippovich: I don't know where he went. Fyodor said he was with Shvonder.

In Preobrazhensky's hand:

Will I have to wait a hundred years for the glazier?

In Darya Petrovna's hand (block letters):

ZINA WENT TO THE STORE, SHE SAID SHE WOULD
BRING HIM.

The dining room felt completely like evening, thanks to the
lamp with the silk shade. The light from the buffet sideboard
fell broken in half – the mirrored panes were taped in an
angled cross from one facet to the other. Filipp Filippovich,
bent over the table, was immersed in the enormous sheet
of the unfolded newspaper. Flashes of lightning distorted
his face and fragmented, broken, grumbling words slipped
through his teeth. He read the notice:

> There is no doubt that he is his illegitimate (as they used
> to say in the rotten bourgeois society) son. That is how
> our pseudo-scientific bourgeoisie amuses itself! Each one
> knows how to occupy seven rooms until the gleaming
> sword of justice shines above him in a red beam.
>
> Shv—r

A balalaika was playing very persistently and with a dashing
agility two rooms away, and the sounds of a clever variation
on 'The Moon Is Shining' mixed in Filipp Filippovich's head
with the words from the newspaper into a hateful mush.
When he finished reading, he spat dryly over his shoulder
and unthinkingly sang through his teeth: "'The moooon
is shining… Shining… the moon is shining…' Pfui… it's
stuck in my brain… damned tune!"

He rang. Zina's face showed between the drapes.

"Tell him it's five o'clock. Time to stop. And call him
here, please."

Filipp Filippovich sat in an armchair by the table. A
brown cigar stub stuck out from between the fingers of his

left hand. By the drapes, leaning against the lintel, one leg behind the other, stood a short man with an unpleasant appearance. The hair on his head was bristly, like shrubs on a ploughed field, and there was unshaven fluff on his face. His brow was astonishingly low. The thick brush of hair began almost directly above the black tassels of his widespread eyebrows.

His jacket, torn under the left arm, was sprinkled with straw, the right knee of the striped trousers was ripped and the left smeared with purple paint. Around his neck, the little man wore a tie of a toxic sky colour with a fake ruby pin. The colour of that tie was so bright that from time to time, shutting his weary eyes, Filipp Filippovich could see in total darkness a blazing torch with a blue flame on the ceiling or the wall. Opening them, he was blinded anew by the sight of patent-leather lace-up shoes with white spats spraying fountains of light from the floor.

"Like galoshes," thought Filipp Filippovich with an unpleasant feeling, sighed, huffed, and began fussing with the cigar that had gone out. The man in the doorway regarded the professor with murky eyes and smoked a *papirosa*,* scattering ash on his shirt front.

The clock on the wall next to the wooden hazel grouse struck five. Something inside the clock was still groaning when Filipp Filippovich embarked on a conversation.

"I believe I've asked you twice now not to sleep on the plank bed by the stove in the kitchen, especially in the daytime?"

The man coughed hoarsely, as if choking on a bone, and replied, "The air is more pleasant in the kitchen."

His voice was unusual, soft yet resonant, as if in a small barrel.

Filipp Filippovich shook his head and asked, "Where did you get that vile thing? I'm speaking of the tie."

The man, following the pointing finger, squinted over his pouting lip and looked lovingly at the tie.

"Why 'vile'?" he said. "It's a fabulous tie. Darya Petrovna gave it to me."

"Darya Petrovna gave you a vile thing. Like those shoes. What is that glowing nonsense? From where? What did I request? Buy de-cent shoes! And what is this? Could Doctor Bormental have picked those out?"

"I told him to get patent leather. What, am I worse than other people? Go out on Kuznetsky, everyone's wearing patent leather."

Filipp Filippovich turned his head and spoke significantly: "Sleeping on the kitchen bed is ended. Understood? What obnoxiousness! You are in the way! There are women there."

The man's face darkened and his lips stuck out.

"Some women! Big deal! Fancy ladies! An ordinary servant and she acts like a commissar. It's that Zinka tattling."

Filipp Filippovich gave him a stern look. "Don't you dare call Zina 'Zinka'! Do you understand?"

Silence.

"Do you understand, I said?"

"I understand."

"Remove that thing from your neck. You... just take a look at yourself in the mirror – you're a sight! A circus act! No throwing butts on the floor, I'm telling you for the hundredth time. I don't want to hear another swear word in the apartment. No spitting. There's the spittoon. Be careful at the urinal. No talking to Zina at all! She complains that you lurk in the dark waiting for her. Watch it! Who told a patient 'The dog only knows'? Do you think you're in a tavern?"

"You're really putting the squeeze on me, Pops," the man said plaintively.

Filipp Filippovich reddened and his spectacles gleamed. "Who here is a 'pops' to you? What familiarity! I never want to hear that word again! Use my name and patronymic when you address me!"

A presumptuous expression flashed in the man. "You and your rules... don't spit, don't smoke... don't go there... What is all this? It's just like being on the tram. Why won't you let me live? And it won't work about the 'pops', you know! Did I ask to have the surgery?" the man barked in outrage. "Fine behaviour! Grabbed an animal, sliced up his head, and now you mock him. Maybe I didn't give my permission for the surgery. And maybe, neither did (the little man looked up at the ceiling, as if trying to recall a formulation), neither did my family. Maybe I have the right to sue."

Filipp Filippovich's eyes grew completely round and the cigar fell from his hands. "What a character!" flew through his mind.

"What," he asked, narrowing his eyes, "you dare to be displeased to have been turned into a human? Perhaps you would prefer to run around the rubbish dump again? Freeze in the alleys? Well, had I but known!"

"Why do you keep berating me with the dump? I was earning my crust! What if I had died under your knife? What do you have to express about that, Comrade?"

"'Filipp Filippovich!'" Filipp Filippovich exclaimed in irritation. "I'm no comrade of yours! This is monstrous!" He thought, "A nightmare, a nightmare!"

"Yes, of course, we understand," said the man ironically and victoriously set his foot back. "We understand! How could we be comrades! No way! We weren't educated in universities or brought up in fifteen-room apartments with bathrooms! But now it is time to drop all that. At the present time, everyone has the right—"

Filipp Filippovich turned pale as he listened to the man's ruminations. The latter interrupted his speech and demonstratively headed towards the ashtray carrying his chewed *papirosa*. He had a swaying gait. He crushed the butt in the tray for a long time, his expression clearly saying: "Take that! And that!" Having put out the *papirosa*, he suddenly clicked his teeth and stuck his nose under his arm.

"Catch fleas with your fingers! Your fingers!" shouted Filipp Filippovich furiously. "And I can't understand where you get them."

"What do you think, that I breed them or something?" The man was insulted. "Apparently, fleas like me," he said, feeling around in the lining under his sleeve and releasing a clump of reddish cotton batting into the air.

Filipp Filippovich turned his gaze to the garlands on the ceiling and drummed his fingers on the table. The man executed the flea and moved away to sit on a chair. He let his hands dangle from the wrists along the lapels of his jacket. His eyes squinted towards the squares of the parquet floor. He was admiring his shoes, which gave him great pleasure. Filipp Filippovich glanced down at the harsh glints of light on the squared toes, narrowed his eyes, and spoke. "What other matter did you want to report to me?"

"Some matter! It's a simple matter. I need a document, Filipp Filippovich."

A nerve twitched on Filipp Filippovich's face.

"Hm... Damn... A document! Really... Hm... Well, maybe it can be avoided somehow?" His voice was unconfident and bleak.

"Oh, please," the man replied confidently. "How can one be without a document? Well, excuse me. You know that a person is strictly forbidden to exist without a document. First of all, the BuildCom!"

"What does this BuildCom have to do with it?"

"What do you mean, what? They run into me, they ask, 'When are you going to register, esteemed one?'"

"Oh, my God," exclaimed Filipp Filippovich drearily. "'Run into you, they ask...' I can imagine what you tell them! Don't forget that I have forbidden you to skulk around the stairs!"

"What am I, a convict?" the man demanded, and the consciousness of his righteousness burned even in his ruby. "What do you mean 'skulk'? Your words are rather offensive! I walk like everyone else."

He slid his patent-leathered feet along the floor.

Filipp Filippovich grew silent and averted his eyes. "I really need to control myself," he thought. He went to the buffet and gulped down a glass of water.

"Fine," he said more calmly, "it's not about the words. So, what does this charming BuildCom of yours say?"

"What is there to say? And you needn't berate it as 'charming'. It defends interests."

"Whose interests, may I enquire?"

"You know whose. The labouring element."

Filipp Filippovich's eyes bulged. "How are you a labourer?"

"You know I'm not a NEPman."*

"Well, all right. Thus, what does it need to defend your revolutionary interests?"

"You know what: register me. They say it's impossible for a man to live in Moscow unregistered. That's one. But the most important thing is a registration card. I don't want to be a deserter. And then, the union, the exchange—"

"Would you please tell me where I'm supposed to register you? On this tablecloth? On my own passport? You have to consider the situation! Don't forget that you... er... hm... you are, so to speak, an unexpected creature, a laboratory..." Filipp Filippovich spoke with dwindling confidence.

The man maintained a victorious silence.

"Excellent. What then is needed, really, in order to register you and generally arrange things according to the plan of this BuildCom of yours? After all, you have no name or surname!"

"You're being unfair. I can select a name for myself quite easily. Just print it in the newspaper, and wham! Presto!"

"And what do you wish to be called?"

The man adjusted his tie and replied, "Polygraf Polygrafovich."

"Stop playing the fool," Filipp Filippovich responded sourly. "I'm being serious with you."

A sarcastic smirk twisted the man's little moustache.

"I seem to be missing something here," he said merrily and meaningfully. "I can't swear, I can't spit, and all I hear from you is 'fool' and 'fool'. Apparently, only professors are allowed to swear in the RSFSR."*

Blood rushed to Filipp Filippovich's head, and as he poured water into a glass, he broke it. Drinking from another, he thought, "A little more and he'll start lecturing me and he'll be absolutely right. I can't control myself anymore."

He bowed with exaggerated politeness and with iron firmness in his voice he said, "For-give me. My nerves are shot. Your name seemed strange to me. I wonder where you dug it up?"

"The BuildCom suggested it. They looked in the calendar,* which one do you want, and I picked it."

"There couldn't be anything of the sort in any calendar."

"That's rather surprising," the man chuckled, "since it's in your examining room."

Filipp Filippovich leant back without getting out of his chair to the button on the wallpaper, and Zina appeared in response to the ring.

"The calendar from the examining room."

A pause ensued. When Zina returned with the calendar, Filipp Filippovich asked, "Where?"

"He's celebrated on 4th March."

"Show me... Hm... damn... Into the stove with it, Zina, right now!"

Zina, eyes bulging in fear, left with the calendar, and the man shook his head reproachfully.

"May I know your surname?"

"I'm willing to take my hereditary surname."

"What? Hereditary? That is?"

"Sharikov."

Chairman of the BuildCom Shvonder, in a double-breasted leather jacket, stood in front of the desk in the study. Doctor Bormental sat in the armchair. The doctor's frost-reddened cheeks (he had just returned) bore the same bewildered expression as Filipp Filippovich.

"What should be written?" he asked impatiently.

"Why," Shvonder said, "it's not complicated. Write an affidavit, Citizen Professor. That, like, the holder of this is indeed Citizen Sharikov, Polygraf Polygrafovich, hm... conceived in your, like, apartment—"

Bormental, surprised, shifted in his chair. Filipp Filippovich's moustache twitched.

"Hm... what the hell... I can't imagine anything stupider than this. He wasn't conceived at all, but simply... well, basically—"

"That's your problem," Shvonder said with calm gloating, "whether he was conceived or not... The whole point is that you did the experiment, Professor! So you created citizen Sharikov."

"It's really simple," barked Sharikov from the bookcase. He was peering at his tie, reflected in the mirrored abyss.

"I would beg you," Filipp Filippovich snarled, "not to interfere in the conversation. You are wrong to say 'It's really simple' – it is really not simple."

"How can I not interfere?" Sharikov muttered in an injured tone, and Shvonder instantly supported him.

"Forgive me, Professor, Citizen Sharikov is completely correct. It is his right to participate in the discussion of his own fate, especially since the matter concerns documents. A document is the most important thing in the world."

At that moment, a deafening ring above his ear broke off the conversation. Filipp Filippovich said into the receiver, "Yes!" reddened and shouted, "I ask that you not distract me with trifles! What's it to you?" And he whipped the receiver into the cradle.

An idyllic joy spread over Shvonder's face.

Filipp Filippovich, turning crimson, shouted, "Let's finish this."

He tore a sheet out of a pad and scribbled a few words, which he read aloud in irritation.

"'I hereby attest'... damned if I know what this is... Hm... 'The bearer is a person, obtained by laboratory experiment

via an operation on the brain, who needs documents'...
Damn!... I am against you obtaining these idiotic documents!... 'Signed: Professor Preobrazhensky.'"

"It's rather strange, Professor," Shvonder said, taking
umbrage, "how can you call documents idiotic? I cannot
allow the habitation in our building of an undocumented
resident, especially one who has not been put on the army
draft list by the police. What if there is a war with imperial-
ist predators?"

"I'm not going to any war," Sharikov barked grimly into
the bookcase.

Shvonder was taken aback but quickly regained his
position and noted obligingly to Sharikov, "You, Citizen
Sharikov, are speaking unconsciously in the highest degree.
You must be on the military list."

"I'll go on the list, but fight – you can go blow," Sharikov
replied with hostility, adjusting the bow.

It was Shvonder's turn to be confused. Preobrazhensky
looked over at Bormental both viciously and sadly, "Fine
morals, eh?" Bormental nodded significantly.

"I was heavily wounded during the operation," Sharikov
whined grimly. "See what they did to me?" He pointed
to his head. A very fresh surgical scar stretched across
his brow.

"Are you an anarchist individualist?" Shvonder asked,
eyebrows rising high.

"I should have a medical exemption," Sharikov responded
to that.

"Well, that's not important right now," replied the
astounded Shvonder. "The fact is that we will send the
professor's affidavit to the police and you will be given a
document."

"Here's the thing, uh…" Filipp Filippovich interrupted, clearly tormented by some thought or other, "would you have a free room in the building? I'm willing to buy it."

Yellow sparks appeared in Shvonder's brown eyes. "No, Professor, to my great regret. No possibility of one."

Filipp Filippovich compressed his lips and said nothing. The phone rang like mad again. Filipp Filippovich, without answering it, silently threw the receiver from the cradle so hard that it spun a bit and then dangled on its light-blue cord. Everyone shuddered.

"The old man's nerves are shot," thought Bormental, while Shvonder, eyes gleaming, bowed and left.

Sharikov, the leather borders of his shoes creaking, followed him out.

The professor was left alone with Bormental. After a short time, Filipp Filippovich shook his head rapidly and began speaking. "It's a nightmare, upon my word. Do you see? I swear, dear Doctor, these last two weeks have been more exhausting than the last fourteen years! He's a character, I'll tell you—"

In the distance, glass smashed softly, then a stifled female scream flew up and immediately went out. An evil spirit raced across the wallpaper in the hallway, heading for the examining room, where something crashed, and instantly flew back again. Doors slammed and Darya Petrovna's low cry resounded in the kitchen. Then Sharikov howled.

"My God! What now!" shouted Filipp Filippovich, rushing to the door.

"A cat," surmised Bormental and rushed out behind him. They ran down the corridor to the entrance, burst in, from there turned down the corridor to the toilet and bathroom.

CHAPTER 6

Zina jumped out of the kitchen and bumped right into
Filipp Filippovich.

"How many times have I given the orders, no cats!"
Filipp Filippovich shouted furiously. "Where is he? Ivan
Arnoldovich, calm down the patients in the reception, for
God's sake!"

"In the bathroom, the damned devil is in the bathroom,"
Zina shrieked, panting.

Filipp Filippovich shoved against the bathroom door, but
it did not yield.

"Open up this second!"

In response, something jumped around the locked bathroom walls, knocking over basins, and Sharikov's wild voice
roared mutedly beyond the door: "I'll kill you on the spot!"

Water rushed through the pipes and poured out. Filipp
Filippovich pushed harder on the door and began tugging at
it. Overheated Darya Petrovna, her face contorted, appeared
in the kitchen doorway. Then the high glass pane, leading
from the bathroom to the kitchen at ceiling level, crashed
with a vermiform crack and two shards fell from it, followed
by a huge cat with tiger stripes and a pale-blue ribbon on
his neck, looking like a policeman. It fell right on the table
onto the long serving dish, which broke in half lengthwise,
leapt from the dish to the floor, then turned on three legs,
raising the right one as if dancing, and instantly squeezed
through a narrow crevice onto the back stairs. The crevice
expanded, and the cat was replaced by an old lady's phizog
in a kerchief. The old woman's skirt, sprinkled with white
polka dots, appeared in the kitchen. The old woman wiped
her concave mouth with her index finger and thumb, cast
her puffy and prickly eyes around the kitchen, and said with
curiosity, "Oh, Lord Jesus!"

Pale Filipp Filippovich crossed the kitchen and asked the old woman sternly, "What do you want?"

"I'd like a look at the talking dog," the old woman replied beseechingly and crossed herself.

Filipp Filippovich grew even paler, came right up to the woman and whispered stiflingly, "Out of this kitchen this second."

The old woman backed towards the door and said in an injured voice, "You're awfully rude, Professor sir."

"Out, I say," repeated Filipp Filippovich, and his eyes grew as round as the owl's. He personally slammed the back door behind the old woman. "Darya Petrovna, haven't I asked you before?!"

"Filipp Filippovich," replied Darya Petrovna in despair, balling up her exposed hands into fists. "What can I do?... People keep trying to barge in all day, I'd have to drop everything else!"

The water in the bathroom roared dull and threatening, but no voices were heard. Doctor Bormental came in.

"Ivan Arnoldovich, I beg you... Hm... how many patients out there?"

"Eleven," Bormental replied.

"Let them all go, I won't see patients today!"

Filipp Filippovich rapped his knuckle on the door and shouted, "Come out this moment! Why have you locked yourself in?"

"Ooo-ooo!" Sharikov's voice was piteous and dull.

"What the hell!... I can't hear you! Turn off the water!"

"Woof... oooo!"

"Turn it off! What has he done? I don't understand!" shrieked Filipp Filippovich in a rage. Zina and Darya Petrovna, mouths agape, stared at the door in despair. A suspicious splashing joined the noise of the rushing water. Filipp Filippovich banged his fist on the door.

"There he is!" called Darya Petrovna from the kitchen.

Filipp Filippovich hurried there. In the broken window by the ceiling, Polygraf Polygrafovich's mug appeared and pushed through into the kitchen. It was contorted, the eyes weepy, and a scratch, flaming with fresh blood, extended along his nose.

"Have you lost your mind?" asked Filipp Filippovich. "Why aren't you coming out?"

Sharikov, also in despair and fear, looked around and replied, "I'm clicked in!"

"Open the lock! What, haven't you ever seen a lock?"

"It won't open, damn it," Polygraf replied fearfully.

"Lordy! He clicked the double lock!" cried Zina and clasped her hands.

"There's a little button," shouted Filipp Filippovich, trying to be heard over the water. "Push it down... Down! Push it down!"

Sharikov vanished and returned to the window in a minute.

"Too dark to see a dog in here," he barked in horror through the window.

"Turn on the light! He's gone mad!"

"Damned cat smashed the lamp," replied Sharikov, "so I started to grab the bastard by the legs, the tap got twisted off and now I can't find it."

All three clasped their hands before them and froze in that position.

About five minutes later, Bormental, Zina and Darya Petrovna were sitting next to each other on a wet rug rolled up at the bottom of the door, using their nether parts to press it against the crack under the door, while Fyodor the doorman, holding Darya Petrovna's wedding candle, climbed up the wooden ladder to the dormer window. His rear end in large grey checks flashed in the air and vanished into the opening.

"Wooof-oooo!" Sharikov shouted something through the roar of the water.

Under pressure, water sprayed a few times onto the kitchen ceiling and then grew still.

Fyodor's voice could be heard: "Filipp Filippovich, we have to open the door anyway, let it flow out, we'll pump it out of the kitchen!"

"Open!" cried Filipp Filippovich angrily.

The troika stood up from the rug, the bathroom door was opened and a wave poured into the hallway. There, it separated into three streams: straight into the toilet opposite, right to the kitchen and left to the entrance. Sloshing and hopping, Zina slammed the door to the entrance. Ankle-deep in water, Fyodor came out, smiling for some reason. He looked as if he had been wrapped in oilcloth – all wet.

"Barely shut it off, the pressure is strong," he explained.

"Where is he?" Filipp Filippovich asked and raised one foot with a curse.

"Afraid to come out," chuckling stupidly, Fyodor explained.

"Will you beat me, Pops?" came Sharikov's whiny voice from the bathroom.

"Idiot!" responded Filipp Filippovich succinctly.

Zina and Darya Petrovna, skirts tucked above the knee and bare-legged, and Sharikov and the doorman, barefoot with pants rolled up, swabbed the kitchen floor with wet rags, which they wrung out into dirty buckets and the sink.

The abandoned stove hummed. Water went out the door to the back stairs right through the staircase, falling into the cellar.

Bormental, standing on tiptoe in a deep puddle on the parquet floor of the entrance, negotiated through the door opened on the chain.

"No doctors' hours today, the professor is unwell. Please, move away from the door, we had a burst pipe."

"When will he receive?" a voice behind the door demanded. "I just need a minute."

"I can't," Bormental said, rocking back from his toes onto his heels. "The professor is lying down, and the pipe is burst. Please, come back tomorrow. Zina, dear! Wipe away from here, otherwise it will pour out onto the front stairs."

"The rags won't take it!"

"We'll bail it out with mugs!" called Fyodor. "Coming!"

The doorbell kept ringing, and now Bormental's whole foot was in the water.

"Then when will the surgery be?" importuned a voice trying to push through the crack.

"The pipe burst."

"I can come in my galoshes."

Bluish silhouettes appeared beyond the door.

"Sorry, come back tomorrow."

"But I have an appointment."

"Tomorrow. We've had a catastrophe with the plumbing."

Fyodor squirmed around at the doctor's feet in the lake, bailing with a mug, while scratched-up Sharikov came up with a new method. He rolled a huge rag into a tube, lay down with his stomach in the water and pushed it from the entrance back towards the bathroom.

"You loon, why are you pushing it all through the apartment?" grumbled Darya Petrovna. "Pour it into the sink!"

"Forget the sink!" Sharikov replied, trying to catch the murky water with his arms. "It will crawl out onto the front stairs."

With a creak, a bench rolled out of the corridor with Filipp Filippovich in blue striped socks stretched out on it, balancing himself.

"Ivan Arnoldovich, stop answering. Go to the bedroom, I'll give you slippers."

"It's all right, Filipp Filippovich, it's nothing!"

"Get galoshes then!"

"Really, it's all right. My feet are wet anyway."

"Oh, my God," said Filipp Filippovich bleakly.

"What a vicious animal," Sharikov grumbled suddenly and came out squatting with a soup bowl in his hand.

Bormental slammed the door and gave in to laughter. Filipp Filippovich's nostrils flared and his glasses glinted.

"You are speaking of whom?" he asked Sharikov from on high. "Permit me to know."

"I'm talking about the cat. What a bastard!" Sharikov replied, eyes wandering.

"You know, Sharikov," Filipp Filippovich responded, after a deep breath, "I have positively never seen a more brazen creature than you."

Bormental giggled.

"You," Filipp Filippovich continued, "are obnoxious! How dare you say that! You are the cause of all this and yet you dare... No! The Devil knows what this is!"

"Sharikov, tell me, please," Bormental asked, "how much longer are you going to chase cats? Shame on you, it's outrageous, you know!"

"Savage!"

"I'm no savage!" Sharikov responded grumpily. "No savage at all. It's impossible to allow him in the apartment. He just looks for something to swipe. He gobbled up Darya's ground meat. I wanted to teach him a lesson."

"You need to be taught a lesson!" replied Filipp Filippovich. "Just look at your mug in the mirror."

"Almost lost an eye," Sharikov responded firmly, touching his eye with a black, wet hand.

When the parquet floor, so soaked it was black, had dried a bit and all the mirrors bore a steam-bath sheen and the doorbell had stopped ringing, Filipp Filippovich stood in the entrance wearing red leather slippers.

"This is for you, Fyodor."

"I thank you humbly."

"Change your clothes immediately. But wait: have Darya Petrovna give you some vodka."

"I thank you humbly." Fyodor shuffled his feet and then said, "There's something else, Filipp Filippovich. I apologize, I feel guilty. But there's the glass in apartment seven... Citizen Sharikov threw rocks..."

"At a cat?" asked Filipp Filippovich, darkening like a cloud.

"As if – at the apartment owner. He's threatening to go to court."

"Damn!"

"Sharikov embraced their cook, and the master started to chase him out... Well, they got into it..."

"Please, always tell me about such things right away. How much do you need?"

"One and half."

Filipp Filippovich fished out three shiny fifty-copeck coins and handed them to Fyodor.

"Having to shell out that much on account of that bastard," came the low voice from the doorway. "It's all his—"

Filipp Filippovich turned, bit his lip, and silently pushed Sharikov into the reception room and locked him in. Sharikov instantly started banging his fists on the door.

"Don't you dare!" Filipp Filippovich cried in a sickly voice.

"Well, that's really something," Fyodor noted meaningfully. "I've never seen anyone so obnoxious in my life!"

Bormental appeared out of nowhere. "Filipp Filippovich, I beg you, stay calm!" The energetic Asclepius* unlocked the door to the reception room, and they could hear his voice coming from there. "What's the matter with you? Do you think you're in a tavern or something?"

"That's the way!" Fyodor added enthusiastically. "That's it! And box his ear too!"

"Now, now, Fyodor," Filipp Filippovich muttered sadly.

"Believe me, I feel sorry for you, Filipp Filippovich."

Chapter 7

"NO, NO, AND NO!" Bormental began insistently. "Please tuck it in!"

"Really, what, honest to God," grumbled Sharikov.

"Thank you, Doctor," Filipp Filippovich said gently, "I've got tired of correcting him."

"I won't let you eat until you tuck it in. Zina, receive the mayonnaise from Sharikov."

"What do you mean, 'receive'?" Sharikov was upset. "I'll tuck it in now."

With his left hand he blocked the dish from Zina and with his right he shoved a napkin inside his collar, coming to resemble someone at the barber's.

"Use the fork, please," Bormental added.

Sharikov gave a long sigh and started fishing for pieces of sturgeon in the thick sauce.

"A little more vodka?" he announced interrogatively.

"Haven't you had enough?" Bormental enquired. "You've been hitting the vodka too much lately."

"Do you begrudge it?" Sharikov enquired and looked up from beneath his brow.

"That's silly," Filipp Filippovich interjected severely, but Bormental interrupted him. "Don't worry, Filipp Filippovich, I'll handle it. You, Sharikov, speak nonsense and the most outlandish thing is that you say it with aplomb and confidence. Of course, I don't begrudge the vodka, especially since it's not even mine but Filipp Filippovich's. It's just that it's harmful. That's one, and two, you behave improperly as it is without it."

Bormental pointed to the taped-up buffet.

"Zina, dear, please give me some more fish."

Sharikov reached for the decanter in the meantime, and with a sidelong glance at Bormental, poured himself a shot.

"You must offer it to others," said Bormental, "and in this way: first to Filipp Filippovich, then to me, and finally for yourself."

A barely visible satirical smile touched Sharikov's lips, and he filled all the shot glasses.

"We have to do everything like on parade," he said. "Napkin here, tie there, and 'excuse me', and 'please', '*merci*', instead of doing it for real. We're tormenting ourselves the way they did under the tsarist regime."

"And what is 'for real', may I enquire?"

Sharikov did not respond to Filipp Filippovich, instead raising his glass and saying, "Here's wishing that everything—"

"And the same to you," Bormental replied with some irony.

Sharikov sloshed the vodka down his throat, frowned, brought a piece of bread to his nose, sniffed it and then swallowed it, his eyes brimming with tears.

"A stage," Filipp Filippovich suddenly said curtly and as if in a trance.

Bormental glanced at him in amazement. "Sorry?"

"A stage!" repeated Filipp Filippovich and shook his head bitterly. "There's nothing to be done about it! Klim!"

Bormental peered with extreme interest into Filipp Filippovich's eyes. "Do you suppose so, Filipp Filippovich?"

"No supposing about it. I'm certain."

"Could it..." began Bormental and stopped, glancing over at Sharikov.

The latter frowned suspiciously.

"*Später*,"* said Filipp Filippovich softly.

"*Gut*," replied his assistant.

Zina brought in the turkey. Bormental poured some red wine for Filipp Filippovich and offered it to Sharikov.

"I don't want any. I'd rather have some vodka." His face looked greasy, sweat beaded his brow, and he was cheerful. Filipp Filippovich also grew kinder after his wine. His eyes were clearer and he regarded Sharikov, whose black head sat in the napkin like a fly in sour cream, with greater condescension.

Bormental, feeling stronger, revealed a tendency towards action. "Well, and what shall we undertake this evening?" he enquired of Sharikov.

He blinked and replied, "We'll go to the circus, that's the best."

"The circus every day?" Filipp Filippovich remarked rather genially. "That's rather boring, it seems to me. If I were you I'd go to the theatre at least once."

"I won't go to the theatre," Sharikov said with hostility and made the sign of the cross over his mouth.*

"Hiccuping at the table spoils the appetite of others," Bormental informed him automatically. "Please forgive me... Why, actually, don't you like the theatre?"

Sharikov looked into his empty shot glass as if it were binoculars, thought, and pouted. "It's tomfoolery... Talk and talk... Nothing but counter-revolution!"

Filipp Filippovich threw himself against the Gothic chair back and laughed so hard that gold palings sparkled in his mouth. Bormental merely shook his head.

"You should read something," he proposed, "otherwise, you know—"

"I'm reading and reading as it is," Sharikov replied and suddenly poured himself half a glass of vodka swiftly, like a predator.

"Zina!" Filipp Filippovich called anxiously. "Take the vodka away, child, we don't need any more! What are you reading?" He had a sudden picture flash through his mind: an uninhabited island, a palm tree, and a man in an animal skin and hat. "You should read Robinson—"

"That ... whatchacallit... correspondence between Engels and that... what's his name, damn it... and Kautsky."*

Bormental's fork with a piece of white meat stopped half-way, and Filipp Filippovich spilt his wine. Sharikov managed to down his vodka in the meantime.

Filipp Filippovich rested his elbows on the table, looked at Sharikov and asked, "Permit me to enquire what you can say in connection with your reading."

Sharikov shrugged.

"I don't agree."

"With whom? Engels or Kautsky?"

"Both of them," Sharikov replied.

"Marvellous, I swear to God! 'All who say another!...'* And what would you propose instead?"

"What's there to propose?... They keep writing and writing... Congress, some Germans... makes my head ache! Just take everything and divide it up."

"Just as I thought!" exclaimed Filipp Filippovich, smacking the tablecloth with his hand, "That's just what I thought!"

"Do you know the method as well?" Bormental asked, intrigued.

"What method?" Sharikov had become more talkative under the influence of the vodka. "It's no secret. Look now: one is spread out over seven rooms, with forty pairs of pants, while another forages, looking for food in rubbish bins."

"The seven rooms is a dig at me, I take it?" Filipp Filippovich asked, narrowing his eyes haughtily. Sharikov huddled into himself and said nothing.

"Well, all right, I'm not against sharing. Doctor, how many patients did you turn away yesterday?"

"Thirty-nine people,' Bormental replied instantly.

"Hm... Three hundred and ninety roubles. Well, let the men bear the damage. We won't count the ladies – Zina and Darya Petrovna. Your share, Sharikov, is one hundred and thirty roubles. Please hand it over."

"A fine thing," replied Sharikov in a fright, "what's all this?"

"For the tap and the cat!" barked Filipp Filippovich, losing his state of ironic calm.

"Filipp Filippovich!" Bormental exclaimed anxiously.

"Wait! For the outrage you created, which made us cancel office hours! It is unacceptable! A man leaping around the apartment, like a savage, tearing off taps!... Who killed Madam Polasukher's cat? Who—"

"You, Sharikov, the other day you bit a lady on the stairs!" attacked Bormental.

"You stand—" growled Filipp Filippovich.

"She smacked me on the face!" screeched Sharikov. "My mug isn't public property!"

"Because you pinched her breast," shouted Bormental, knocking over his wine glass. "You stand—"

"You stand on the lowest step of development!" Filipp Filippovich out-shouted him. "You are a creature still in formation, weak mentally, all your actions are purely animal, and you, in the presence of two people with a university education, permit yourself with totally unbearable aplomb to offer advice of cosmic scale and equally cosmic stupidity on dividing everything up, and at the same time you gobbled up the tooth powder!"

"The other day," Bormental confirmed.

"So now," thundered Filipp Filippovich, "I will rub your nose in this… by the way, why did you wipe off the zinc oxide from it?… You will be silent and listen to what you are told! Learn and try to become at least a minimally acceptable member of society. By the way, what scoundrel outfitted you with that book?"

"You think everyone's a scoundrel," Sharikov replied fearfully, overwhelmed by the two-sided attack.

"I can guess!" exclaimed Filipp Filippovich, wrathfully turning red.

"Well, all right, then… Well, it was Shvonder. He's not a scoundrel. For my development—"

"I can see how you're developing after Kautsky," Filipp Filippovich shrieked, turning yellow. He furiously pushed the button on the wall. "Today's incident shows that better than anything! Zina!"

"Zina!" yelled Bormental.

"Zina!" screamed frightened Sharikov.

Zina ran in, pale.

"Zina, in the reception room… Is it in the reception room?"

"In the reception," Sharikov replied docilely. "Green, like vitriol."

"A green book—"

"He's going to fire off now!" Sharikov exclaimed in despair. "It's not mine, it's from the library!!"

"The correspondence is called... what's his name? .. Engels with that devil... Into the stove with it!"

Zina turned and flew out.

"I would hang that Shvonder from the nearest tree, upon my word," Filipp Filippovich exclaimed, furiously clamping his teeth into a turkey wing, "this incomparable rotten creature exists in the building like a boil. It's not enough that he writes libellous nonsense in the papers..."

Sharikov squinted angrily and ironically at the professor. Filipp Filippovich in turn glared narrowly at him and stopped talking.

"Oh, nothing good will come of us here in the apartment," Bormental suddenly thought prophetically.

Zina brought in a round tray holding a baba, reddish on the right side and rosy on the left, and the coffee pot.

"I won't eat that," Sharikov announced in a threatening and hostile way.

"No one's asking you to. Behave yourself. Doctor, please."

The dinner ended in silence.

Sharikov pulled a crumpled *papirosa* from his pocket and lit up. Finishing his coffee, Filipp Filippovich looked at his watch, pressed the chimes, and they tenderly played quarter-past eight. Filipp Filippovich leant back on the Gothic chair as was his habit and reached for the newspaper on the side table.

"Doctor, please, take him to the circus. But, for God's sake, check the programme – are there any cats?"

"How can they let that kind of riff-raff into the circus," Sharikov noted grimly, shaking his head.

"They let all sorts in," Filipp Filippovich replied ambiguously. "What are they playing?"

"At Solomonovsky's," Bormental started reading, "there are four of these... Yussems and some kind of spinning man."

"What are Yussems?" Filipp Filippovich enquired suspiciously.

"God knows, I've never seen the word before."

"Well, then, you'd better see what Nikitin has. Everything must be clear."

"Nikitin... Nikitin... hm... Elephants and the extreme of human agility."

"Sooooo. What do you have to say regarding elephants, dear Sharikov?" Filipp Filippovich asked Sharikov doubtfully.

He was offended. "What, you think I don't understand, is that it? Cats are different, but elephants are useful animals," Sharikov replied.

"Fine then. If they're useful, then go and see them. You must obey Ivan Arnoldovich. And do not get into any conversations at the buffet. Ivan Arnoldovich, I humbly entreat you not to offer beer to Sharikov."

Ten minutes later, Ivan Arnoldovich and Sharikov, dressed in a duckbill cap and thick woollen overcoat with the collar turned up, left for the circus. It grew quiet in the apartment. Filipp Filippovich appeared in his study. He lit the lamp under the heavy green hood, which made the enormous study very peaceful, and started pacing the room.

The cigar tip burned long and hot with a pale-green fire. The professor tucked his hands into his trouser pockets and a heavy thought tormented his learned brow with its widow's peak. He smacked his lips, hummed, "To the sacred banks of the Nile," and muttered something.

At last, he set the cigar in the ashtray, went over to the cupboard that was completely made of glass, and illuminated the entire study with three powerful lights from the ceiling. From the third glass shelf in the cupboard, Filipp Filippovich removed a narrow jar and examined it, frowning, holding it up to the light. In the transparent and viscous liquid there floated, without sinking to the bottom, a small white lump, excised from the depths of Sharikov's brain. Shrugging, twisting his lips and hemming, Filipp Filippovich devoured it with his eyes, as if trying to find in the white, unsinkable lump the cause of the astonishing events that had turned life upside down in the apartment on Prechistenka.

It is quite possible that the scholarly man did find it. At least, having regarded to his content the appendage of the brain, he put away the jar, locked the cupboard, placed the key in his vest pocket and collapsed, tucking his head into his shoulders and sticking his hands deep into his jacket pocket, onto the leather of the couch. He burned a second cigar for a long time, chewing up its tip, and finally, in total solitude, coloured green like a grey-haired Faust, he exclaimed: "I swear to God, I think I'll do it!"

No one responded. All sounds had ceased in the apartment. Traffic stops in Obukhov Lane at eleven, as you know. Once in a great while the distant footsteps of a late pedestrian could be heard, thumping somewhere beyond the drapes, and then dying away. The pocket-watch chimes rang gently beneath Filipp Filippovich's fingers in his pocket. The professor waited impatiently for Doctor Bormental and Sharikov to return from the circus.

Chapter 8

I T's NOT KNOWN what Filipp Filippovich had decided
to do. He did not undertake anything special in the
course of the week and perhaps, in consequence of his
inaction, everyday life in the apartment was overwhelm-
ingly eventful.

About six days after the business with the water and the
cat, the young man who turned out to be a woman from
the BuildCom came to Sharikov and handed him documents, which Sharikov immediately placed in his jacket
pocket and just as immediately afterwards called Doctor
Bormental.

"Bormental!"

"Oh, no, you use my name and patronymic with me,
please!" replied Bormental, face contorted.

It should be noted that in those six days the surgeon
managed to argue some eight times with his charge, and
the atmosphere was sticky in the rooms on Obukhov Lane.

"Then you use my name and patronymic," Sharikov
replied quite reasonably.

"No!" thundered Filipp Filippovich in the doorway. "I will
not permit you to be called by that name and patronymic.
If you prefer not to be called familiarly as 'Sharikov', then
Doctor Bormental and I will call you 'Mr Sharikov'."

"I'm not a mister, the misters are all in Paris," barked
Sharikov.

"Shvonder's work!" shouted Filipp Filippovich. "Well, fine then, I'll deal with that scoundrel. There will be nothing but misters in my apartment as long as I live here! Otherwise, either you or I will leave here, and most likely that will be you! Today I will place an advertisement in the papers, and believe me, I'll find you a room!"

"Right, like I'm stupid enough to move from here," Sharikov replied very clearly.

"What?" demanded Filipp Filippovich and his face changed so much that Bormental rushed over and tenderly and anxiously took him by the sleeve.

"Don't you take liberties, Monsieur Sharikov." Bormental's voice was raised very high. Sharikov stepped back, pulled three papers from his pocket – green, yellow and white – and jabbing his fingers at them, said, "There. I'm a member of the residence association, and I'm assigned thirty-five square feet of space in apartment number five of the responsible renter Preobrazhensky." Sharikov thought and added an expression that Bormental mechanically noted as new: "Be so kind."

Filipp Filippovich bit his lip and carelessly muttered through it, "I swear that I will end up shooting that Shvonder."

Sharikov took those words extremely attentively and acutely, as was apparent from his eyes.

"Filipp Filippovich, *vorsichtig*,"* Bormental began to caution him.

"Really, that's too... To stoop so low!" exclaimed Filipp Filippovich in Russian. "Bear in mind, Sharikov... Mr... that if you permit yourself one more obnoxious statement, I will deprive you of dinner and any board at all in my house. Thirty-five feet is delightful, but those froggish papers don't oblige me to feed you, do they?"

Sharikov was frightened and opened his mouth. "I can't stay without board," he muttered. "Where will I get grub?"

"Then behave yourself decently," both Asclepiuses howled as one.

Sharikov was significantly subdued and that day caused no harm to anyone except himself: using Bormental's brief absence, he appropriated his razor and ripped open his cheekbone so that Filipp Filippovich and Doctor Bormental had to give him stitches, which made Sharikov howl for a long time, weeping copiously.

The next night, two men sat in the professor's study in the dim green light – Filipp Filippovich and his loyal and devoted Bormental. Everyone else was asleep. Filipp Filippovich wore his azure robe and red slippers and Bormental was in shirtsleeves with blue suspenders. Between the doctors, the round table held a thick album, a bottle of brandy, a plate of lemon slices* and a cigar box. The scientists, having filled the room with smoke, were heatedly discussing the latest events: that evening Sharikov had stolen two ten-rouble notes lying under a paperweight from Filipp Filippovich's study, vanished from the apartment, returned late and completely drunk. More than that, he came back with two unknown characters who made noise on the front stairs and expressed their desire to spend the night as Sharikov's guests. The signified characters left only when Fyodor, who was present at this scene in his autumn coat thrown over his underwear, called the forty-fifth police station. The characters left the moment Fyodor hung up. With their departure, the malachite ashtray from the mirror shelf in the entrance, Filipp Filippovich's beaver hat and his walking stick, inscribed in gold with: "To dear and esteemed Filipp Filippovich from his grateful orderlies on the day…" followed by the Roman numeral XXV, went missing somewhere.

"Who are they?" Filipp Filippovich threatened Sharikov, making fists.

Swaying and sticking to the fur coats, he muttered that he did not know those characters and that they weren't some sons of bitches but good fellows.

"The most amazing part is that they were both drunk, how did they manage?" wondered Filipp Filippovich, regarding the spot on the stand where once stood the memorial of his anniversary.

"Specialists," explained Fyodor, heading back to bed with a rouble in his pocket.

Sharikov categorically and stubbornly denied the two ten-rouble notes and said something unclear about the fact that, like, he's not the only one in the apartment.

"Aha, perhaps it was Doctor Bormental who swiped the money?" enquired Filipp Filippovich in a voice quiet yet terrible in its tone.

Sharikov reeled, opened his completely owlish eyes and offered a suggestion: "Maybe Zinka took it."

"What!" screamed Zina, appearing in the doorway like a ghost, covering the unbuttoned blouse on her chest with her palms. "How dare he—"

Filipp Filippovich's neck turned red. "Easy, Zinusha," he said, extending a hand towards her. "Don't worry, we will take care of all this."

Zina immediately started wailing, blubbering, and her hand jumped up and down on her collarbone.

"Zina! Shame on you! Who could possibly think that? Pfui, how vile," Bormental said in confusion.

"Really, Zina, you're stupid, God forgive me," Filipp Filippovich began. But Zina's weeping stopped of its own accord and everyone stopped talking. Sharikov was feeling sick. Hitting his head on the wall, he emitted a sound – not quite "ee" and not quite "eh" – like "eee-eh"! His face paled and his jaw worked convulsively.

"The bucket from the examining room for the scoundrel!"

Everyone ran around, taking care of the sick Sharikov. When they took him to bed, he stumbled in Bormental's arms and cursed very delicately and melodically with swear words, pronouncing them with difficulty.

This whole business had occurred around one o'clock, and now it was around three, but the two men in the study were wide awake, agitated by the brandy. They had smoked so much that the smoke moved in thick, slow layers without any swaying.

Doctor Bormental, pale, with a very determined gaze, raised a glass with a wasp waist. "Filipp Filippovich!" he exclaimed emotionally, "I'll never forget how I came to you, a half-starved student, and you sheltered me in the faculty. Believe me, Filipp Filippovich, you are much more to me than my teacher, my professor... My unlimited respect for you... Permit me to kiss you, dear Filipp Filippovich."

"Yes, my dear fellow, my..." Filipp Filippovich muttered in bewilderment and rose to meet him. Bormental embraced him and kissed him in his fluffy, heavily smoky moustache.

"I swear to God, Filipp Fili—"

"I'm so touched, so touched... thank you," Filipp Filippovich said. "My dear fellow, I sometimes shout at you during surgery. Do forgive an old man's irritability. Essentially, I am so alone... 'From Seville to Granada...'"

"Filipp Filippovich, you should be ashamed!" exclaimed fiery Bormental sincerely. "If you do not wish to offend me, do not speak to me in that manner."

"Well, thank you… 'To the sacred banks of the Nile!'… Thank you. And I've come to love you as a talented physician."

"Filipp Filippovich, I'm telling you," Bormental cried passionately, leapt from his chair, shut the door leading to the corridor more tightly, and continued in a whisper when he returned, "it's the only way. I don't dare give you advice, of course, but Filipp Filippovich, look at yourself, you're completely exhausted, you can't work any more!"

"Absolutely impossible!" Filipp Filippovich confirmed with a sigh.

"There, it's just unthinkable," whispered Bormental. "The last time you said that you were worried for me, and if you only knew how much that touched me, dear Professor. But I'm not a boy and I understand myself how terribly it might turn out. But, I profoundly believe that there is no other way."

Filipp Filippovich rose, waved his arms at him and exclaimed, "Don't tempt me, don't even say it." The professor paced the room, setting off smoky waves. "I won't even listen. You realize what will happen if we're discovered. We won't get off because 'class origins are taken into account', despite a previous conviction. We don't have the right origins, do we, dear boy?"

"Not in the least! My father was a judicial investigator in Vilno," Bormental replied bitterly, finishing his cognac.

"There, that won't do. It's a bad heredity. Can't even think of anything more disgusting. Actually, my mistake, mine's even worse. My father was an archpriest in a cathedral.

Merci... 'From Seville to Granada in the quiet twilight...'
Damn it all!"

"Filipp Filippovich, you are a luminary of world significance, and over some son of a bitch, pardon the expression... They wouldn't dare touch you, believe me!"

"All the more reason why I won't do it," Filipp Filippovich
responded thoughtfully, stopping and looking at the glass
cupboard.

"Why not?"

"Because you aren't a luminary of world significance."

"Far from it..."

"Exactly. But abandoning a colleague in case of catastrophe while getting out of it myself using my world significance, sorry... I am a Moscow student, not a Sharikov."
Filipp Filippovich proudly straightened his shoulders and
looked like an ancient French king.

"Filipp Filippovich, ah!" Bormental exclaimed bitterly.
"Then what now? Put up with it? You're going to wait until
we manage to turn that hooligan into a man?"

"Ivan Arnoldovich, in your opinion, do I understand a
little in the anatomy and physiology of, say, the apparatus
of the human brain? What do you think?"

"Filipp Filippovich, how can you ask!" Bormental replied
with great feeling and opened his arms.

"Fine, then. Without false modesty. I also think that I'm
not the last person in that area in Moscow."

"I think that you are the first, and not only in Moscow, but
in London and Oxford too!" Bormental interrupted fiercely.

"Fine, so be it. But then listen, future Professor Bormental:
No one can do it. No need to ask. Just use me as a refer-
ence. Tell them, Preobrazhensky said so. *Finita*! Klim!"
Filipp Filippovich suddenly exclaimed triumphantly, and

the cupboard responded with ringing panes. "Klim!" he repeated. "Here's the thing, Bormental, you're the best student in my school and besides that my friend, as I have become convinced today. So I am telling you a secret as a friend – of course I know that you will not shame me, how the old ass Preobrazhensky screwed up this operation like a third-year student. Of course, there was the discovery, you know that for yourself" – and here Filipp Filippovich pointed bitterly with both hands at the window shade, apparently indicating Moscow – "but just bear in mind, Ivan Arnoldovich, that the only result of this discovery will be that now we all will have that Sharikov up to here." Preobrazhensky patted himself on his bent neck, which had a tendency towards paralysis. "Don't worry! If someone," Filipp Filippovich continued voluptuously, "were to lay me down and give me a whipping, I swear I would pay him fifty roubles! 'From Seville to Granada…' Damn me… I spent five years digging out appendages from brains… Do you know what kind of work I did, it's mind-boggling. And now I ask, for what? So that one fine day I could turn a sweet dog into scum that makes your hair stand on end!"

"Something exceptional."

"I don't agree at all. This is what happens, Doctor, when a researcher doesn't feel his way in parallel with nature but forces the issue and raises the curtain! Here, have your Sharikov and eat him with buckwheat!"

"Filipp Filippovich, what if it had been Spinoza's brain?"*

"Yes!" barked Filipp Filippovich. "Yes! If only the miserable dog doesn't die under the knife, and you've seen what sort of operation it is. In other words, I, Filipp Preobrazhensky, have never done anything harder in my life. One can transplant Spinoza's pituitary or that of some other supernatural creature and create from a dog something extremely high on the scale, but what the devil for, I ask? Explain to me, please, why we need to artificially fabricate Spinozas, when any peasant woman can give birth to one whenever!... After all, Mrs Lomonosov gave birth to her famous son in Kholmogory.* Doctor, humanity takes care of this itself, and in the evolutionary process, stubbornly separating out from the mass of all kinds of scum, it creates dozens of outstanding geniuses who ornament the globe. Now you see, Doctor, why I denigrated your conclusion in Sharikov's case history. My discovery, may the devils take it, which you think is so wonderful, isn't worth a plugged copeck... Don't argue, Ivan Arnoldovich, I've figured it out. I never waste my breath, you know that perfectly well. Theoretically, it is interesting, yes. Physiologists will be delighted... Moscow is in an uproar... But, practically, what do we have? Whom do you see before you?" Preobrazhensky pointed in the direction of the examining room, where Sharikov slept.

"An exceptional rascal."

"But who is he? Klim, Klim," shouted the professor, "Klim Chugunkin!" (Bormental's mouth fell open.) "Here is what that is: two convictions, alcoholism, 'divide up everything', my hat and twenty roubles missing (here Filipp Filippovich recalled his anniversary walking stick and turned red) – a lout and a pig... Well, I'll find that stick. In other words, the pituitary gland is a closed chamber that determines a person's given character. Given! 'From Seville to Granada...'" Filipp Filippovich shouted, eyes rolling furiously, "And not generally human! It is the brain itself in miniature! I don't need it at all, the hell with it! I was concerned with something completely different: eugenics, improving the human race. And I came across rejuvenation! Do you really think that I regenerate them for the money? I am a scientist, after all—"

"You are a great scientist, so there," said Bormental, gulping brandy. His eyes were bloodshot.

"I wanted to do a small experiment after I first extracted sex hormone from the pituitary two years ago. And instead of that, what has happened, oh my God! All those hormones in the pituitary, oh Lord… Doctor, I am facing a dead end of hopelessness, I swear I am lost."

Bormental suddenly rolled up his sleeves and said, squinting at his nose, "Then here's the thing, dear teacher, if you do not wish to do it, I will feed him arsenic at my own risk. The hell with the fact that my father was a judicial investigator. After all, it's your own experimental creature."

Filipp Filippovich calmed down, weakened, collapsed into his chair and said, "No, I will not permit it, dear boy. I am sixty years old, I can give you advice. Never commit a crime, no matter against whom. Live to an old age with clean hands."

"But my goodness, Filipp Filippovich, if that Shvonder works on him some more, think what he'll turn into? God, I'm only beginning to realize what that Sharikov could become!"

"Aha! Now you understand? I realized it ten days after the operation. But see here, Shvonder is the greatest fool of all. He doesn't realize that Sharikov is a much graver threat to him than to me. Right now, he's trying everything to pit him against me, without realizing that if someone decides to pit Sharikov against Shvonder, there will be nothing left of him but his horns and hooves."

"Just think of the cats! A man with a dog's heart!"

"Oh, no, no," Filipp Filippovich drew out his words. "You are making an enormous mistake, Doctor – for God's sake, don't calumny the dog. The cats are just temporary... It's a question of discipline and two or three more weeks. I assure you. In a month or so he'll stop attacking them."

"But why not now?"

"Ivan Arnoldovich, it's elementary, are you really asking? The pituitary isn't going to just hang in the air. It's grafted onto a dog's brain, after all; give it time to take. Sharikov is now manifesting only the remnants of the canine, and don't forget that the cats are the best of what he's been doing. You must realize that the true horror is that he no longer has a dog's heart but a human one. The worst of all of those that exist in nature."

Agitated to the extreme, Bormental tightened his strong, thin hands into fists, straightened his shoulders, and stated firmly, "It's over. I'll kill him!"

"I forbid it!" Filipp Filippovich was categorical.

"Please—"

Filipp Filippovich looked up warily, raising his finger. "Wait... I heard footsteps."

They both listened, but it was quiet in the corridor.

"I imagined it," said Filipp Filippovich and spoke heatedly in German. The Russian word "criminality" sounded several times in his speech.

"Just a minute," Bormental suddenly said and stepped towards the door. Steps could be heard clearly, moving toward the study. In addition, a voice mumbled. Bormental flung open the doors and jumped back in astonishment. Completely stunned, Filipp Filippovich froze in his chair.

In the illuminated rectangle of the hallway, Darya Petrovna in just her nightgown stood with a militant and blazing face. The doctor and the professor were blinded by the abundance of the powerful and, as it seemed to the startled men, completely naked body. With her mighty arms, Darya Petrovna was dragging something, and that something resisted, sitting on its rear, and its small legs, covered with black fluff, struggled on the floor. The something was of course Sharikov, completely lost, still tipsy, dishevelled and in his night shirt.

Darya Petrovna, magnificent and naked, shook Sharikov like a sack of potatoes and said these words: "Take a look, Professor sir, at our visitor Telegraf Telegrafovich. I've been married, but Zina is an innocent girl. It's a good thing that I woke up."

Finishing this speech, Darya Petrovna fell into a state of shame, cried out, covered her bosom with her hands and rushed away.

"Darya Petrovna, forgive me, for Heaven's sake!" red-faced Filipp Filippovich, rousing himself, called after her.

Bormental rolled his shirtsleeves higher and moved on Sharikov.

Filipp Filippovich, seeing his eyes, was horrified. "Doctor! I forbid it."

Bormental grabbed Sharikov by the back of his shirt with his right hand and shook him so hard that the fabric on the back cracked and a button from the neck in front broke off.

Filipp Filippovich tried to head him off and began pulling scrawny Sharikov out of the tenacious surgical hands.

"You don't have the right to fight," half-stifled Sharikov shouted, sitting down on the floor and sobering up.

"Doctor!" screamed Filipp Filippovich,

Bormental came to his senses a bit and released Sharikov, who immediately started sobbing.

"Fine, then," hissed Bormental. "We'll wait until morning. I'll throw him a special benefit performance when he sobers up."

Then he grabbed Sharikov under his arms and dragged him to the reception room to sleep. Sharikov made an attempt to kick him away, but his legs would not obey.

Filipp Filippovich spread his feet, thus separating the azure skirts of his robe, raised his arms and eyes to the ceiling lamp in the corridor and said, "Well-well-well."

Chapter 9

THE SPECIAL PERFORMANCE for Sharikov promised by Doctor Bormental did not take place, however, the next morning because Polygraf Polygrafovich had vanished from the house. Bormental was infuriated and despairing, called himself an ass for not hiding the key to the front door, shouted that this was unforgivable, and ended with the hope that Sharikov would be hit by a bus. Filipp Filippovich sat in his study, hands in his hair, saying, "I can just imagine what will happen on the street... I can ima-a-gine. 'From Seville to Granada', oh, my God."

"He might still be in the BuildCom office," Bormental raged and ran off somewhere.

At the office he got into such an argument with chairman Shvonder that the latter sat down to write a complaint to the People's Court of Khamovnichesky District, shouting that he was not the keeper of Professor Preobrazhensky's ward, especially since that ward Polygraf no later than last night proved to be a fraud who took seven roubles from the committee allegedly to buy textbooks at the co-op store.

Fyodor, who had made three roubles on this incident, searched the house from top to bottom. There was no trace of Sharikov.

The only thing they learnt was that Polygraf had left at dawn wearing cap, scarf and coat, taking a bottle of ash-berry vodka from the buffet, Doctor Bormental's gloves and all his documents. Darya Petrovna and Zina did not conceal their turbulent joy and hope that Sharikov would never return. Sharikov had borrowed three roubles and fifty copecks from Darya Petrovna the day before.

"Serves you right!" roared Filipp Filippovich, brandishing his fists.

The telephone rang all day, and the telephone rang the next day. The doctors saw an unusual number of patients, and on the third day the question arose firmly in the study about informing the police, who would have to find Sharikov in the whirlpool that was Moscow.

No sooner was the word "police" pronounced than the reverential quiet of Obukhov Alley was sundered by the barking of a truck, and the windows of the house shook. Then came a confident peal of the bell, and Polygraf Polygrafovich appeared in the entrance. Both the professor and the doctor came out to meet him.

Polygraf entered with extraordinary dignity, removed his cap in total silence, hung his coat on the coat rack and stood before them in a new guise. He wore a second-hand leather jacket, worn leather pants and tall English boots that laced to the knee. Preobrazhensky and Bormental, as if given a command, crossed their arms on their chests and stood in the doorway, awaiting the first announcement from Polygraf Polygrafovich.

He smoothed his bristly hair, coughed and looked around, showing that Polygraf wanted to hide his embarrassment by overfamiliarity.

"I, Filipp Filippovich," he began at last, "have taken a position."

Both doctors made a vague dry sound in the throat and stirred.

Preobrazhensky was first to rouse himself and he reached out and said, "Give me the paper."

It read: "The bearer Comrade Polygraf Polygrafovich Sharikov is indeed head of the Subdepartment for Control of Moscow's Stray Animals (cats and so on) in the Department of Moscow Communal Administration."

"So," said Filipp Filippovich heavily, "who found you the job? Ah, actually, I can guess..."

"Well, Shvonder," replied Sharikov.

"Permit me to enquire why you give off that disgusting reek?"

Sharikov worriedly sniffed his jacket.

"Well, what can I do, it smells... obviously. From my speciality. Yesterday we killed and killed cats."

Filipp Filippovich shuddered and looked at Bormental. His eyes were like two black pistol barrels pointed directly at Sharikov. Without any preamble, he moved towards Sharikov and easily and confidently took him by the throat.

"Help!" Sharikov squeaked, turning pale.

"Doctor!"

"I won't do anything bad, Filipp Filippovich, don't worry," Bormental replied in a steely voice and then shouted, "Zina and Darya Petrovna!"

They appeared in the entrance.

"Repeat after me," said Bormental and pushed Sharikov's throat slightly towards the fur coat. "Forgive me..."

"All right, I'm repeating," Sharikov, completely vanquished, replied in a hoarse voice, and then suddenly took a deep breath, jerked away and tried to shout, "Help!" but the shout did not come out and his head was completely engulfed by the coat.

"Doctor, I beg you!"

Sharikov nodded to show that he was submitting and would repeat.

"…Forgive me, esteemed Darya Petrovna and Zinaida—"

"Prokofyevna," Zina whispered in fright.

"Prokofyevna," Sharikov said hoarsely, gasping for air.

"…that I permitted myself…"

"…permitted…"

"…vile behaviour at night in a state of intoxication…"

"…intoxication…"

"I will never do it again…"

"…will ne—"

"Let him go, let him go, Ivan Arnoldovich," both women entreated simultaneously. "You'll choke him!"

Bormental released Sharikov and said, "Is the truck waiting for you?"

"No," Polygraf replied respectfully. "It just brought me here."

"Zina, tell the car to leave. Now bear this in mind: you have returned to Filipp Filippovich's apartment?"

"Where else could I go?" Sharikov replied meekly, eyes darting.

"Fine. Keep quiet, lie low. Otherwise, you will have me to deal with for every outrageous act. Understood?"

"Understood," Sharikov replied.

Filipp Filippovich had said nothing during the violence on Sharikov. He had huddled pathetically near the door lintel and chewed on his nail, gaze directed at the floor. Then he looked up at Sharikov and asked, softly and mechanically, "What do you do with those… killed cats?"

"They'll go to make coats," Sharikov said. "They'll turn into 'squirrel' for worker credit."

Thereupon, silence descended upon the apartment and continued for two days. Polygraf Polygrafovich left in the morning by truck, returned in the evening, dined quietly in the company of Filipp Filippovich and Bormental. Despite the fact that Bormental and Sharikov slept in the same room, the reception, they did not speak to each other, and Bormental was first to tire of it.

About two days later, a thin young lady wearing eyeliner and cream stockings appeared in the apartment and was truly overwhelmed by its opulence. In her shabby coat she followed Sharikov and bumped into the professor in the entrance.

He stopped, stunned, squinted and asked, "May I be informed?"

"I'm registering marriage with her; she's our typist, she'll live with me. Bormental will have to move out of the reception room, he has his own apartment," Sharikov explained with extreme hostility and grumpiness.

Filipp Filippovich blinked, thought as he regarded the red-faced young lady, and spoke to her very courteously, "I'll ask you to come into my study for a minute."

"I'll go with her," Sharikov said quickly and suspiciously.

The decisive Bormental popped up instantly, as if from under the floor.

"Excuse me," he said. "The professor will chat with the lady, and you and I will wait here."

"I don't want to," Sharikov replied angrily, trying to follow the young lady, burning with shame, and Filipp Filippovich.

"No, sorry." Bormental took Sharikov by the arm and they went to the examining room.

For about five minutes, no sounds were heard from the study and then suddenly came the muffled sound of the young lady's weeping.

Filipp Filippovich stood by his desk, and the young lady cried into a dirty lace hankie.

"He said, the louse, that he was wounded in combat," the young lady sobbed.

"He's lying," Filipp Filippovich replied intransigently. He shook his head and continued, "I feel sincere sympathy for you, but really you can't just go off with the first person you meet, just for the sake of your job... Child, it's outrageous... Now here."

He opened a desk drawer and took out three thirty-rouble notes.

"I'll get food poisoning," the young lady wept. "The canteen serves salt beef every day... He threatened me, says he's a red commander... with me, he says, you'll live in a luxurious apartment... pineapple every day... my psyche is kind, he says, it's only cats I hate... he took my ring for a keepsake."

"Well, well, well, a kind psyche... 'From Seville to Granada'," muttered Filipp Filippovich. "You'll get over this, you're so young."

"Was it really in this very alley?"

"Come on, take money when it's offered, a loan," snapped Filipp Filippovich.

Then the doors were opened ceremoniously, and Bormental, at Filipp Filippovich's signal, brought in Sharikov. His eyes darted around, and the pelt on his head bristled like a brush.

"Scoundrel," said the young lady, flashing her puffy, smeared eyes and stripy powdered nose.

"Do explain to this lady why you have a scar on your forehead," Filipp Filippovich asked ingratiatingly.

Sharikov bet the house. "I was wounded at the front fighting Kolchak,"* he barked.

The young lady stood and left with a loud cry.

"Stop!" Filipp Filippovich called after her. "Wait! The ring," he said to Sharikov.

He obediently removed the hollow ring with an emerald.

"All right now," he said angrily to her, "you're in for it now. Tomorrow I'll arrange to have you fired!"

"Don't be afraid of him!" Bormental shouted after her. "I won't let him do anything." He turned and gave Sharikov a look that made him back away and bang his head on the cupboard.

"What's her surname?" Bormental asked him. "Her name!!!" he screamed, suddenly looking savage and terrifying.

"Vasnetsova," replied Sharikov, looking around for an escape route.

"Every day," Bormental said, holding the lapel of Sharikov's jacket, "I will personally enquire about staff reductions, whether Citizen Vasnetsova has been fired. And if you... if I find out that she's been fired, I will shoot you with my own hands that very moment! Watch it, Sharikov, I'm speaking to you in plain Russian!"

Sharikov stared at Bormental's nose.

"We'll find our own revolvers," Polygraf muttered, but very weakly, and then suddenly twisted away and shot out the door.

"Watch it!" Bormental's cry caught up with him.

That night and half the next day, silence hung in the air like a cloud before a storm. But everyone was silent. But the next day, when Polygraf Polygrafovich, who had felt a bad premonition that morning, left gloomily for work in the truck, Professor Preobrazhensky, at a totally unofficial time, saw one of his previous patients, a fat and tall man in military uniform. He had insisted on an appointment and got it. Entering the study, he clicked his heels politely.

"Have your pains returned, dear fellow?" asked the haggard Filipp Filippovich. "Sit down please."

"*Merci*. No, Professor," his visitor replied, placing his helmet at the corner of the desk, "I'm very grateful to you. Um... I'm here for something else, Filipp Filippovich... With my great respect... hm... To warn you. It's blatant nonsense. He's just a scoundrel."

The patient dug into his briefcase and took out a piece of paper. "It's a good thing they reported it to me directly."

Filipp Filippovich saddled his nose with pince-nez over his glasses and started reading. He muttered to himself for a long time, his face changing expression every second.

"...and also threatened to kill Chairman of the BuildCom Comrade Shvonder, which shows that he has firearms. And he makes counter-revolutionary speeches and even ordered his social servant Zinaida Prokofyevna Bunina to burn Engels in the stove, as a blatant Menshevik with his assistant Ivan Arnoldovich Bormental, who without being registered lives secretly in his apartment. I certify the signature of Head of the Animal Control Subdepartment P.P. Sharikov. Chairman of BuildCom Shvonder, Secretary Pestrukhin."

"May I keep this?" asked Filipp Filippovich, all blotchy, "or, forgive me, perhaps you need this to set legal machinery in action?"

"Excuse me, Professor," said the patient in great offence, nostrils flaring, "you really do have a very scornful view of us. I—" and here he started puffing up like a turkey cock.

"Forgive me, forgive me, dear fellow," muttered Filipp Filippovich, "forgive me, truly I did not wish to insult you."

"We know how to read papers, Filipp Filippovich!"

"Dear fellow, don't be angry, he's driven me to distraction."

"I can imagine," the patient said, completely calm again. "But what scum he is! I'd be curious to see him. There are all sorts of legends going around Moscow about you."

Filipp Filippovich merely waved off the suggestion in despair. And here the patient saw that the professor had grown stooped and even seemed to have turned grey over recent months.

The crime ripened and fell like a stone, as it usually happens. With a festering feeling in his heart, Polygraf Polygrafovich returned in the truck. Filipp Filippovich's voice called him into the examining room. Surprised, Sharikov entered and with a vague fear looked at the gun barrels on Bormental's face and then at Filipp Filippovich. A dark cloud circled the assistant and his left hand, holding a cigarette, trembled on the shiny arm of the obstetric chair.

Filipp Filippovich said with very nasty calm, "Gather up your things now: trousers, coat, everything you need, and get out of the apartment."

"What do you mean?" Sharikov was truly surprised.

"Get out today," Filipp Filippovich repeated in a monotone, squinting at his fingernails.

Some evil spirit had entered Polygraf Polygrafovich; apparently disaster was waiting for him and fate was behind his back. He threw himself into the embrace of the inevitable and barked angrily and curtly, "What is this, really! Do you think I won't find a way to deal with you? I'm sitting on thirty-five feet here and I'm staying."

"Get out of the apartment," Filipp Filippovich whispered with feeling.

Sharikov invited his death. He raised his left hand and made a rude gesture with his bitten and cat-stinking finger at Filipp Filippovich. And then with his right hand, addressed to the dangerous Bormental, he took a revolver from his pocket. Bormental's *papirosa* dropped like a falling star and a few seconds later, Filipp Filippovich, horrified and jumping over broken glass, was rushing between the cupboard and the couch. There, prostrate and gasping, lay the head of the Animal Control Subdepartment, and on his chest was the surgeon Bormental, smothering him with a small white pillow.

A few minutes later, Doctor Bormental, his face unrecognizable, went to the front door and put up a sign next to the bell: "No patients today because the professor is ill. Please do not disturb by ringing the bell."

He used his shiny penknife to cut through the bell's wires, and then he examined his scratched, bloody face and his torn hands, jittering with a rapid tremor, in the mirror. Then he appeared in the kitchen doorway and in a cautious voice said to Zina and Darya Petrovna, "The professor asks that you do not leave the apartment."

"All right," replied Zina and Darya Petrovna meekly.

"Allow me to lock the back door and take the key," said Bormental, hiding in the shadows behind the door and covering his face with his hand. "It's temporary, and not out of lack of trust in you. But if someone comes, you won't be able to resist and you'll open up, and we can't be disturbed. We're busy."

"All right," the women replied and immediately turned pale.

Bormental locked the back door, locked the front door, locked the door from the corridor to the entrance, and then his steps vanished near the examining room.

Silence covered the apartment, crept into all the corners. Twilight crawled in, nasty, wary; in a word, gloom.

Of course, later the neighbours across the court-yard maintained that allegedly all the lights were on in Preobrazhensky's examining-room windows, which open on the yard, and that they even saw the professor's white cap...

Checking this is difficult. Of course, even Zina, when it was all over, gabbed that in the study, by the fireplace, after Bormental and the professor left the examining room, Ivan Arnoldovich had scared her to death. Allegedly he was crouched in the study by the fire burning his own notebook with the blue cover out of the pile in which he kept the case histories of the professor's patients. The doctor's face was allegedly completely green and completely, really completely scratched to bits. And Filipp Filippovich that night was not himself. And also... However, it's also possible that the naive girl from the apartment on Prechistenka is lying...

But one thing is definitely true. That night the apartment was filled with total and terrible quiet.

Epilogue

E XACTLY TEN NIGHTS AFTER the battle in the examining room in the apartment of Professor Preobrazhensky, which is located in Obukhov Alley, the bell rang sharply.

"Criminal police and investigator. Please open up."

Steps sounded, rang out, started to enter and lots of people ended up in the entrance, sparkling with lights and newly glassed-in cupboards. Two in police uniform, one in a black coat with a briefcase, gloating and pale chairman Shvonder, the youth who was a girl, the doorman Fyodor, Zina, Darya Petrovna and half-dressed Bormental, shyly covering his tieless throat.

The door from the study let Filipp Filippovich pass through. He came in his azure robe, known to all, and everyone could see right away that Filipp Filippovich had put back on a lot of weight in the past week. The former imperious and energetic Filipp Filippovich, full of dignity, stood before his nocturnal guests and apologized for his robe.

"Don't be discomfited, Professor," replied the man in civilian dress in great embarrassment, then he hummed and hawed and spoke again. "It's very unpleasant... We have an order to search your apartment and an" – the man looked at Filipp Filippovich's moustache and finished up – "an arrest warrant, depending on the results."

Filipp Filippovich narrowed his eyes and asked, "And on what charges, may I ask, and whom?"

The man scratched his cheek and started to read from a paper in briefcase: "Charging Preobrazhensky, Bormental, Zinaida Bunina and Darya Ivanova with the murder of the Head of Animal Control Subdepartment of the Department of Moscow Communal Administration, Polygraf Polygrafovich Sharikov."

Zina's sobs covered up the last of his words. There was a movement.

"I don't understand a thing," Filipp Filippovich replied, majestically rolling his shoulders. "Who is this Sharikov? Ah, sorry, you mean my dog... the one on which I operated?"

"Excuse me, Professor, not a dog, but when he was already a man. That's the issue."

"You mean, because he spoke?" Filipp Filippovich asked. "That doesn't mean being human! Of course, it's not important. Sharik is alive, and certainly no one killed him."

"Professor," said the man in black in great surprise, raising his eyebrows, "then you will have to produce him. It's ten days since he went missing, and the facts, forgive me, look very bad."

"Doctor Bormental, be so kind as to produce Sharik for the investigator," commanded Filipp Filippovich, taking the arrest warrant in hand.

Doctor Bormental grinned crookedly and left. When he returned and whistled, a dog of strange quality ran in after him through the study door. Some spots were bare, some spots had regrown fur. He came out like a trained circus animal, on his hind legs, then got down on all fours and looked around. Deadly silence congealed in the entrance, like jelly.

The nightmarish dog, with a crimson scar on his forehead, got back up on his hind legs, smiled, and sat in a chair.

The second policeman crossed himself with sweeping gestures and as he moved back stepped on both of Zina's feet.

The man in black, without shutting his mouth, managed to say, "How can this be?... He worked in the Control..."

"I didn't appoint him there," replied Filipp Filippovich. "Mr Shvonder gave him the recommendation, if I'm not mistaken."

"I don't understand," the man in black said in bewilderment and turned to the first policeman. "Is that him?"

"Him," the policeman replied soundlessly. "Him all right."

"The very one," Fyodor's voice spoke out. "But the bastard is overgrown again."

"And he spoke?... Cough, cough."

"He speaks even now, but less and less, so take advantage of the moment before he stops completely."

"But why?" the man in black enquired softly.

Filipp Filippovich shrugged. "Science does not yet know ways to turn animals into people. I tried but unsuccessfully, as you see. He spoke for a while and then started turning back into his original state. Atavism."

"Don't use rude words!" the dog barked from the chair and got up.

The man in black suddenly turned pale, dropped his briefcase, and began to fall sideways, the policeman caught him on the side and Fyodor from behind. A bustle ensued and three voices were clearly audible.

Filipp Filippovich: "Valerian. He's fainted."

Doctor Bormental: "I will personally throw Shvonder down the stairs if he ever shows up in Professor Preobrazhensky's apartment!"

And Shvonder: "Make sure that's on the record!"

* * *

The pipes played their grey harmonies. The drapes hid the thick Prechistenka night with its lone star. The highest creature, the important canine philanthropist sat in an armchair, while the dog Sharik flopped on the rug by the leather couch. The March fog gave the dog headaches in the morning, the pain circling along the seam on his head. But by evening the warmth made them pass. And now it was getting better and better, and pliant and warm thoughts flowed in the dog's head.

"I was so lucky, so lucky," he thought, dozing off, "indescribably lucky. I've established myself in this apartment. I'm definitely sure that something's off in my origins. That Newfoundland is to blame. My grandmother was a slut, may she rest in peace, the old thing. Of course, they've sliced up my head for some reason, but that will heal in time. There's nothing for us to look at there."

In the distance, flasks tinkled softly. The bitten one was tidying the cupboards in the examining room.

The grey-haired magician was sitting and singing, "To the sacred banks of the Nile."

The dog had seen terrible things. The important man plunged his hands wearing slippery gloves into a vessel, taking out brains. The stubborn man persisted, always seeking, cutting, examining, squinting and singing:

"To the sacred banks of the Nile..."

Moscow, January-March 1925

Notes

p. 4, *Celeste Aida*: 'Heavenly Aida', the aria sung by the Egyptian warrior Radames, expressing his love for the Ethiopian slave Aida, from the opera of the same name by Giuseppe Verdi (1813–1901).

p. 5, *chocolates, and bottles of Abrau-Durso*: Chocolates and domestic Champagne-style wine from the northern Caucasus were the height of luxury for a mid-level Soviet bureaucrat.

p. 6, *Sharik*: A typical name for a dog in Russia, the equivalent of Fido.

p. 7, *the fancy stores on Okhotny Ryad*: A square outside the Kremlin in Moscow whose luxury shops symbolized excess; they were torn down in the 1920s and in 1935 replaced by the Moskva Hotel.

p. 13, *a tubby, double-sided bitch of a letter that didn't stand for anything he knew*: The Cyrillic letter F looks like this: Ф; the word being spelt out is "Professor".

p. 16, *From Seville to Granada… in the quiet twilight of the nights*: The opening lines of the romance *Don Juan's Serenade* by Tchaikovsky, based on the poem by Alexei Tolstoy.

p. 19, *Parole d'honneur*: Word of honour (French).

p. 20, *Zhirkost*: A contraction for "State Fat and Bone-rendering Works", a factory which also manufactured cosmetics.

p. 27, *Isadora Duncan*: A pioneering and extravagant figure in modern dance, Isadora Duncan (1877–1927) had strong connections with the USSR, moving to Russia for a short period in 1922, when she married Soviet poet Sergei Yesenin (1895–1925).

p. 32, *The Gardens of Semiramide*: Semiramide was a legendary Assyrian queen, also known as Semiramis II, for whom the Hanging Gardens of Babylon were supposedly built.

p. 33, *The newly blessed*: The Chairman of the People's Commissars, Alexei Rykov (1881–1938), blessed the introduction of a new vodka with a lower alcoholic content.

p. 33, *zakuski for vodka*: Russians accompany vodka with *zakuski*, appetizers. The Slavyansky Bazaar, a celebrated Moscow restaurant (and the scene of Stiva Oblonsky's sumptuous banquet in *Anna Karenina*), was known for a special appetizer: roasted bone marrow served in toasted rye-bread cups.

p. 36, *Karl Marx*: German philosopher and revolutionary socialist (1818–83).

p. 37, *What is this ruination of yours? An old hag with a crutch*: Preobrazhensky is referring to a one-act play by Valery Yazvitsky (1883–1957), *Who Is to Be Blamed? (Ruination)*, performed by the Moscow Studio of Communist Drama in the early 1920s; the main character was an old witch named Ruination, who interfered in the life of a family of a free proletarian.

p. 38, *when he beats the world revolution, Engels and Nikolai Romanov*: Friedrich Engels (1820–95), revered with Karl Marx as a founder of the world revolution, and Tsar Nicholas II (1868–1918), the last emperor of Russia.

p. 42, *Professor Mechnikov*: Ilya Mechnikov (1845–1916), Nobel laureate biologist, who worked in immunology and gerontology and had an interest in rejuvenation.

p. 43, *Muir's*: Muir and Mirrielees, established in Moscow in the 1880s. Today it is known as TsUM and is a high-end fashion department store.

p. 46, *To the sacred banks of the Nile*: The militant and inspiring priests' chorus from *Aida*.

p. 51, *sella turcica*: Also known as the "Turkish saddle", the *sella turcica* is the part of the skull which holds the pituitary gland.

p. 65, *Oh, little apple*: A popular folk ditty from the Civil War era (1917–23), primarily associated with the navy.

p. 66, *Mendeleyev the chemist*: Dmitri Mendeleyev (1834–1907), creator of the periodic table.

p. 71, *smoked a papirosa*: Primarily smoked in Russia, the papirosa's long cardboard tube serves as the holder for the small cigarette attached to the end.

p. 75, *a NEPman*: NEP, the New Economic Policy instituted by Lenin in 1921, was also known as state capitalism; the men who quickly got rich in this short-lived return to capitalism were known as NEPmen.

p. 76, *the RSFSR*: The Russian Soviet Federative Socialist Republic, the largest of the republics of the Soviet Union.

p. 77, *They looked in the calendar*: Russians frequently named their newborn children after the saint venerated on that day in the Orthodox calendar; Shvonder helped Sharikov make a selection from a post-revolutionary calendar, the Day of the Printer (*poligrafist* in Russian).

p. 88, *Asclepius*: The Greek god of medicine.

p. 91, *Später*: "Later" (German).

p. 91, *made the sign of the cross over his mouth*: A folk superstition to keep the Devil from entering the body during a hiccup.

p. 92, *correspondence between Engels and... Kautsky*: Karl Kautsky (1854–1938) was a prominent Czech-German Marxist.

p. 92, *All who say another*: Lyrics from *Don Juan's Serenade* (text by Alexei Tolstoy, music by Pyotr Tchaikovsky), one of the songs for voice and piano.

p. 99, *vorsichtig*: "Careful" (German).

p. 100, *a bottle of brandy, a plate of lemon slices*: Russians traditionally munch on lemon slices, often sprinkled with sugar, when drinking Armenian brandy. Lemon slices topped with sugar and finely ground coffee are known as Nikolashkas, after Nicholas II, who is said to have introduced the custom.

p. 105, *Spinoza's brain*: Baruch Spinoza (1632–77), Dutch rationalist philosopher.

p. 106, *Mrs Lomonosov gave birth to her famous son in Kholmogory*: Mikhail Lomonosov (1711–65), born to a peasant family in the north of Russia, became Russia's iconic polymath: chemist, physicist, astronomer, geographer and poet.

p. 116, *I was wounded at the front fighting Kolchak*: Alexander Kolchak (1874–1920), admiral and leader of the anti-Communist White forces during the Russian Civil War.

Extra Material

on

Mikhail Bulgakov's

A Dog's Heart

Mikhail Bulgakov's Life

Mikhail Afanasyevich Bulgakov was born in Kiev – then in the Russian Empire, now the capital of independent Ukraine – on 15th May 1891. He was the eldest of seven children – four sisters and three brothers – and, although born in Ukraine, his family were Russians, and were all members of the educated classes – mainly from the medical, teaching and ecclesiastical professions. His grandfathers were both Russian Orthodox priests, while his father lectured at Kiev Theological Academy. Although a believer, he was never fanatical, and he encouraged his children to read as widely as they wished, and to make up their own minds on everything. His mother was a teacher and several of his uncles were doctors.

Birth, Family Background and Education

In 1906 his father became ill with sclerosis of the kidneys. The Theological Academy immediately awarded him a full pension, even though he had not completed the full term of service, and allowed him to retire on health grounds. However, he died almost immediately afterwards.

Every member of the Bulgakov family played a musical instrument, and Mikhail became a competent pianist. There was an excellent repertory company and opera house in Kiev, which he visited regularly. He was already starting to write plays which were performed by the family in their drawing room. He was a conservative and a monarchist in his school days, but never belonged to any of the extreme right-wing organizations of the time. Like many of his contemporaries, he favoured the idea of a constitutional monarchy as against Russian Tsarist autocracy.

A few years after her first husband's death, Mikhail's mother married an uncompromising atheist. She gave the children supplementary lessons in her spare time from her own teaching job and, as soon as they reached adolescence, she encouraged them to take on younger pupils to increase the family's meagre income. Mikhail's first job, undertaken when he was still at school, was as a part-time guard and ticket inspector on the local railway, and he continued such part-time employment when he entered medical school in Kiev in 1911.

He failed the exams at the end of his first year, but passed the resits a few months later. However, he then had to repeat his entire second year; this lack of dedication to his studies was possibly due to the fact that he was already beginning to write articles for various student journals and to direct student theatricals. Furthermore, he was at this time courting Tatyana Lappa, whom he married in 1913. She came from the distant Saratov region, but had relatives in Kiev, through whom she became acquainted with Bulgakov. He had already begun by this time to write short stories and plays. Because of these distractions, Bulgakov took seven years to complete what was normally a five-year course, but he finally graduated as a doctor in 1916 with distinction.

War   In 1914 the First World War had broken out, and Bulgakov enlisted immediately after graduation as a Red Cross volunteer, working in military hospitals at the front, which involved carrying out operations. In March 1916 he was called up to the army, but was in the end sent to work in a major Kiev hospital to replace experienced doctors who had been mobilized earlier. His wife, having done a basic nursing course by this time, frequently worked alongside her husband.

In March 1917 the Tsar abdicated, and the Russian monarchy collapsed. Two forces then began to contend for power – the Bolsheviks and the Ukrainian Nationalists. Although not completely in control of Ukraine, the latter declared independence from the former Tsarist Empire in February 1918, and concluded a separate peace deal with Germany. The Germans engineered a coup, placed their own supporters at the helm in Ukraine and supported this puppet regime against the Bolsheviks, the now deposed Nationalists and various other splinter groups fighting for their own causes. The Government set up its own German-supported army, the White Guard, which provided the background for Bulgakov's novel of the same name. The Bolsheviks ("The Reds"), the White Guard ("The Whites") and the Ukrainian Nationalists regularly took and retook the country and Kiev from each other: there were eighteen changes of government between the beginning of 1918 and late 1919.

Early in this period Bulgakov had been transferred to medical service in the countryside around the remote town of Vyazma, which provided him with material for his series of short stories

A Young Doctor's Notebook. Possibly to blunt the distress caused to him by the suffering he witnessed there, and to cure fevers he caught from the peasants he was tending, he dosed himself heavily on his own drugs, and rapidly became addicted to morphine. When his own supplies had run out, he sent his wife to numerous pharmacies to pick up new stocks for imaginary patients. When she finally refused to acquiesce in this any further, he became abusive and violent, and even threatened her with a gun. No more mention is made at any later date of his addiction, so it is uncertain whether he obtained professional help for the problem or weaned himself off his drug habit by his own will-power.

He returned to Kiev in February 1918 and set up in private practice. Some of the early stories written in this period show that he was wrestling with problems of direction and conscience: a doctor could be pressed into service by whichever faction was in power at that moment; after witnessing murders, torture and pogroms, Bulgakov was overwhelmed with horror at the contemporary situation. He was press-ganged mainly by the right-wing Whites, who were notoriously anti-Semitic and carried out most of the pogroms.

Perhaps as a result of the suffering he had seen during his *Turning to* enforced military service, he suffered a "spiritual crisis" – as *Literature* an acquaintance of his termed it – in February 1920, when he gave up medicine at the age of twenty-nine to devote himself to literature. But things were changing in the literary world: Bulgakov's style and motifs were not in tune with the new proletarian values which the Communists, in the areas where they had been victorious, were already beginning to inculcate. The poet Anna Akhmatova talked of his "magnificent contempt" for their ethos, in which everything had to be subordinated to the creation of a new, optimistic mentality which believed that science, medicine and Communism would lead to a paradise on earth for all, with humanity reaching its utmost point of development.

He continued to be pressed into service against his will. Although not an ardent right-winger, he had more sympathy for the Whites than for the Reds, and when the former, who had forced him into service at the time, suffered a huge defeat at the hands of the Communists, evidence suggests that Bulgakov would rather have retreated with the right-wing faction, and maybe even gone into emigration, than have to work for the victorious Communists. However, he was prevented from doing this as just at this time he became seriously ill with typhus, and so remained behind when the Whites fled. Incidentally, both his brothers had fled abroad, and were by this time living in Paris.

From 1920 to 1921 Bulgakov briefly worked in a hospital in the Caucasus, where he had been deployed by the Whites, who finally retreated from there in 1922. Bulgakov, living in the town of Vladikavkaz, produced a series of journalistic sketches, later collected and published as *Notes on Shirt Cuffs*, detailing his own experiences at the time, and later in Moscow. He avowedly took as his model classic writers such as Molière, Gogol and particularly Pushkin, and his writings at this time attracted criticism from anti-White critics, because of what was seen as his old-fashioned style and material, which was still that of the cultured European intellectuals of an earlier age, rather than being in keeping with the fresh aspirations of the new progressive proletarian era inaugurated by the Communists. The authorities championed literature and works of art which depicted the life of the masses and assisted in the development of the new Communist ethos. At the time, this tendency was still only on the level of advice and encouragement from the Government, rather than being a categorical demand. It only began to crystallize around the mid-1920s into an obligatory uncompromising line, ultimately leading to the repression, under Stalin, of any kind of even mildly dissident work, and to an increasingly oppressive state surveillance.

In fact, although never a supporter of Bolshevism as such, Bulgakov's articles of the early 1920s display not approval of the Red rule, but simply relief that at last there seemed to be stable government in Russia, which had re-established law and order and was gradually rebuilding the country's infrastructure. However, this relief at the new stability did not prevent him producing stories satirizing the new social order; for instance, around this time he published an experimental satirical novella entitled *Crimson Island*, purporting to be a novella by "Comrade Jules Verne" translated from the French. It portrayed the Whites as stereotypical monsters and was written in the coarse, cliché-ridden agitprop style of the time – a blatant lampoon of the genre.

But by 1921, when he was approaching the age of thirty, Bulgakov was becoming worried that he still had no solid body of work behind him. Life had always been a struggle for him and his wife Tatyana, but he had now begun to receive some money from his writing and to mix in Russian artistic circles. After his medical service in Vladikavkaz he moved to Moscow, where he earned a precarious living over the next few years, contributing sketches to newspapers and magazines, and lecturing on literature. In January 1924 he met the sophisticated, multilingual Lyubov Belozerskaya, who was the wife of a journalist. In comparison with her, Tatyana seemed provincial and uncultured. They started a relationship, divorced their respective partners, and were entered in the local registers as married in late spring 1924, though the exact date of their marriage is unclear.

Between 1925 and 1926 Bulgakov produced three anthologies of his stories, the major one of which received the overall title *Diaboliad*. This collection received reasonably favourable reviews. One compared his stories in *Diaboliad* to those of Gogol, and this was in fact the only major volume of his fiction to be published in the USSR during his lifetime. According to a typist he employed at this time, he would dictate to her for two or three hours every day, from notebooks and loose sheets of paper, though not apparently from any completely composed manuscript.

But in a review in the newspaper *Izvestiya* of *Diaboliad* and some of Bulgakov's other writings in September 1925, the Marxist writer and critic Lev Averbakh, who was to become head of RAPP (the Russian Association of Proletarian Writers) had already declared that the stories contained only one theme: the uselessness and chaos arising from the Communists' attempts to create a new society. The critic then warned that, although Soviet satire was permissible and indeed requisite for the purposes of stimulating the restructuring of society, totally destructive lampoons such as Bulgakov's were irrelevant, and even inimical to the new ethos.

The Government's newly established body for overseeing literature subsequently ordered *Diaboliad* to be withdrawn, although it allowed a reissue in early 1926. By April 1925, Bulgakov was reading his long story *A Dog's Heart* at literary gatherings, but finding it very difficult to get this work, or anything else, published. In May 1926, Bulgakov's flat was searched by agents of OGPU, the precursor of the KGB. The typescript of *A Dog's Heart* and Bulgakov's most recent diaries were confiscated; the story was only published in full in Russian in 1968 (in Germany), and in the USSR only in 1987, in a literary journal.

In 1926 Bulgakov had written a stage adaptation of the story, but again it was only produced for the first time in June 1987, after which it became extremely popular throughout the USSR.

The White Guard   Between 1922 and 1924 Bulgakov was engaged in writing his first novel, ultimately to be known as *The White Guard*. The publishing history of this volume – which was originally planned to be the first part of a trilogy portraying the whole sweep of the Russian Revolution and Civil War – is extremely complex, and there were several different redactions. The whole project was very important to him, and was written at a period of great material hardship. By 1925 he was reading large sections at literary gatherings. Most of the chapters were published as they were produced, in literary magazines, with the exception of the ending, which was banned by the censors; pirated editions, with concocted endings, were published abroad. The novel appeared finally, substantially rewritten and complete, in 1929 in Paris, in a version approved by the author. Contrary to all other Soviet publications of this period, which saw the events of these years from the point of view of the victorious Bolsheviks, Bulgakov described that time from the perspective of one of the enemy factions, portraying them not as vile and sadistic monsters, as was now the custom, but as ordinary human beings with their own problems, fears and ideals.

It had a mixed reception; one review found it inferior to his short stories, while another compared it to the novelistic debut of Dostoevsky. It made almost no stir, and it's interesting to note that, in spite of the fact that the atmosphere was becoming more and more repressive as to the kind of artistic works which would be permitted, the party newspaper *Pravda* in 1927 could write neutrally of its "interesting point of view from a White-Guard perspective".

First Plays   Representatives of the Moscow Arts Theatre (MAT) had heard Bulgakov reading extracts from his novel-in-progress at literary events, realized its dramatic potential, and asked him to adapt the novel for the stage. The possibility had dawned on him even before this, and it seems he was making drafts for such a play from early 1925. This play – now known as *The Days of the Turbins* – had an extremely complicated history. At rehearsals, Bulgakov was interrogated by OGPU. MAT forwarded the original final version to Anatoly Lunacharsky, the People's Commissar for Education, to verify whether it was sufficiently innocuous politically for them to be able to stage it. He wrote back declaring it was rubbish from an artistic point of view, but as far as subject matter went there was no problem. The theatre seems to have agreed with him as to the literary merit of the piece, since they encouraged the author to embark on an extensive revision, which would ultimately produce a radically different version.

During rehearsals as late as August 1926, representatives of OGPU and the censors were coming to the theatre to hold lengthy negotiations with the author and director, and to suggest alterations. The play was finally passed for performance, but only at MAT – no productions were to be permitted anywhere else. It was only allowed to be staged elsewhere, oddly enough, from 1933 onwards, when the party line was being enforced more and more rigorously and Stalin's reign was becoming increasingly repressive. Rumour had it that Stalin himself had quite enjoyed the play when he saw it at MAT in 1929, regarded its contents as innocuous, and had himself authorized its wider performances.

It was ultimately premiered on 26th October 1926, and achieved great acclaim, becoming known as "the second Seagull", as the first performance of Chekhov's Seagull at MAT in 1898 had inaugurated the theatre's financial and artistic success after a long period of mediocrity and falling popularity. This was a turning point in the fortunes of MAT, which had been coming under fire for only performing the classics and not adopting styles of acting and subject matter more in keeping with modern times and themes. The play was directed by one of the original founders of MAT, Konstantin Stanislavsky, and he authorized a thousand-rouble advance for the playwright, which alleviated somewhat the severe financial constraints he had been living under.

The play received mixed reviews, depending almost entirely on the journal or reviewer's political views. One critic objected to its "idealization of the Bolsheviks' enemies", while another vilified its "petit-bourgeois vulgarity". Others accused it of using means of expression dating from the era of classic theatre which had now been replaced in contemporary plays by styles – often crudely propagandistic – which were more in tune with the Soviet proletarian ethos. The piece was extremely popular, however, and in spite of the fact that it was only on in one theatre, Bulgakov could live reasonably well on his share of the royalties.

At this time another Moscow theatre, the Vakhtangov, also requested a play from the author, so Bulgakov gave them *Zoyka's Apartment*, which had probably been written in late 1925. It was premiered on 28th October, just two days after *The Days of the Turbins*. The theatre's representatives suggested a few textual (not political) changes, and Bulgakov first reacted with some irritation, then acknowledged he had been overworked and under stress, due to the strain of the negotiations with OGPU and the censors over *The Days of the Turbins*.

Various other changes had to be made before the censors were satisfied, but the play was allowed to go on tour throughout the Soviet Union. It is rather surprising that it was permitted, because, in line with party doctrine, social and sexual mores were beginning to become more and more puritanical, and the play brought out into the open the seamier side of life which still existed in the workers' paradise. Zoyka's apartment is in fact a high-class brothel, and the Moscow papers had recently reported the discovery in the city of various such establishments, as well as drug dens. The acting and production received rave reviews, but the subject matter was condemned by some reviewers as philistine and shallow, and the appearance of scantily clad actresses on stage was excoriated as being immoral.

The play was extremely successful, both in Moscow and on tour, and brought the author further substantial royalties. Bulgakov was at this time photographed wearing a monocle and looking extremely dandified; those close to him claimed that the monocle was worn for genuine medical reasons, but this photograph attracted personal criticism in the press: he was accused of living in the past and being reactionary.

Perhaps to counteract this out-of-touch image, Bulgakov published a number of sketches in various journals between 1925 and 1927 giving his reminiscences of medical practice in the remote countryside. When finally collected and published posthumously, they were given the title *A Young Doctor's Notebook*. Although they were written principally to alleviate his financial straits, the writer may also have been trying to demonstrate that, in spite of all the criticism, he was a useful member of society with his medical knowledge.

Censorship   Bulgakov's next major work was the play *Escape* (also translated as *Flight*), which, according to dates on some of the manuscript pages, was written and revised between 1926 and 1928. The script was thoroughly rewritten in 1932 and only performed in the USSR in 1957. The play was banned at the rehearsal stage in 1929 as being not sufficiently "revolutionary", though Bulgakov claimed in bafflement that he had in fact been trying to write a piece that was more akin to agitprop than anything he'd previously written.

Escape is set in the Crimea during the struggle between the Whites and Reds in the Civil War, and portrays the Whites as stereotypical villains involved in prostitution, corruption and terror. At first it seems perplexing that the piece should have been banned, since it seems so in tune with the spirit of the times, but given Bulgakov's well-known old-fashioned and anti-Red stance, the play may well have been viewed as in fact a satire on the crude agitprop pieces of the time.

The year 1929 was cataclysmic both for Bulgakov and for other Soviet writers: by order of RAPP (Russian Association of Proletarian Writers) *Escape*, *The Days of the Turbins* and *Zoyka's Apartment* had their productions suspended. Although, with the exception of *Zoyka*, they were then granted temporary runs, at least until the end of that season, their long-term future remained uncertain.

Bulgakov had apparently started drafting his masterpiece *The Master and Margarita* as early as 1928. The novel had gone through at least six revisions by the time of the writer's death in 1940. With the tightening of the party line, there was an increase in militant, politically approved atheism, and one of the novel's major themes is a retelling of Christ's final days, and his victory in defeat – possibly a response to the atheism of Bulgakov's time. He submitted one chapter, under a pseudonym, to the magazine *Nedra* in May 1929, which described satirically the intrigues among the official literary bodies of the time, such as RAPP and others. This chapter was rejected. Yevgeny Zamyatin, another writer in disfavour at the time, who finally emigrated permanently, stated privately that the Soviet Government was adopting the worst excesses of old Spanish Catholicism, seeing heresies where there were none.

In July of that year Bulgakov wrote a letter to Stalin and other leading politicians and writers in good standing with the authorities, asking to be allowed to leave the USSR with his wife; he stated in this letter that it appeared he would never be allowed to be published or performed again in his own country. His next play, *Molière*, was about problems faced by the French playwright in the period of the autocratic monarch

Louis XIV; the parallels between the times of Molière and the Soviet writer are blatant. It was read in January 1930 to the Artistic Board of MAT, who reported that, although it had "no relevance to contemporary questions", they had now admitted a couple of modern propaganda plays to their repertoire, and so they thought the authorities might stretch a point and permit Bulgakov's play. But in March he was told that the Government artistic authorities had not passed the piece. MAT now demanded the return of the thousand-rouble advance they had allowed Bulgakov for *Escape*, also now banned; furthermore the writer was plagued by demands for unpaid income tax relating to the previous year. None of his works were now in production.

Help from Stalin

On Good Friday Bulgakov received a telephone call from Stalin himself promising a favourable response to his letter to the authorities, either to be allowed to emigrate, or at least to be permitted to take up gainful employment in a theatre if he so wished. Stalin even promised a personal meeting with the writer. Neither meeting nor response ever materialized, but Bulgakov was shortly afterwards appointed Assistant Director at MAT, and Consultant to the Theatre of Working Youth, probably as a result of some strings being pulled in high places. Although unsatisfactory, these officially sanctioned positions provided the writer with some income and measure of protection against the torrent of arbitrary arrests now sweeping through the country.

Yelena
Shilovskaya

Although there was now some stability in Bulgakov's professional life, there was to be another major turn in his love life. In February 1929 he had met at a friend's house in Moscow a woman called Yelena Shilovskaya; she was married with two children, highly cultured, and was personal secretary at MAT to the world-famous theatre director Vladimir Nemirovich-Danchenko. They fell in love, but then did not see each other again for around eighteen months. When they did meet again, they found they were still drawn to each other, divorced their partners, and married in October 1932. She remained his wife till his death, and afterwards became the keeper of his archives and worked tirelessly to have his works published.

Over the next few years Bulgakov wrote at least twice more to Stalin asking to be allowed to emigrate. But permission was not forthcoming, and so Bulgakov would never travel outside the USSR. He always felt deprived because of this and sensed something had been lacking in his education. At this time, because of his experience in writing such letters, and because of his apparent "pull" in high places, other intellectuals such as Stanislavsky and Anna Akhmatova were asking for his help in writing similar letters.

While working at MAT, Bulgakov's enthusiasm quickly waned and he felt creatively stifled as his adaptations for the stage of such classic Russian novels as Gogol's *Dead Souls* were altered extensively either for political or artistic reasons. However, despite these changes, he also provided screenplays for mooted films of both *Dead Souls* and Gogol's play *The Government Inspector*. Once again, neither ever came to fruition. There were further projects at this time for other major theatres, both in Moscow and Leningrad, such as an adaptation of Tolstoy's novel *War and Peace* for the stage. This too never came to anything. In May 1932 he wrote: "In nine days' time I shall be celebrating my forty-first birthday... And so towards the conclusion of my literary career I've been forced to write adaptations. A brilliant finale, don't you think?" He wrote numerous other plays and adaptations between then and the end of his life, but no new works were ever produced on stage.

Things appeared to be looking up at one point, because in October 1931 *Molière* had been passed by the censors for production and was accepted by the Bolshoi Drama Theatre in Leningrad. Moreover, in 1932, MAT had made a routine request to be allowed to restage certain works, and to their surprise were permitted to put *Zoyka's Apartment* and *The Days of the Turbins* back into their schedules. This initially seemed to herald a new thaw, a new liberalism, and these prospects were enhanced by the dissolution of such bodies as RAPP, and the formation of the Soviet Writers' Union. Writers hitherto regarded with suspicion were published.

However, although *Molière* was now in production at the Leningrad theatre, the theatre authorities withdrew it suddenly, terrified by the vituperative attacks of a revolutionary and hard-line Communist playwright, Vsevolod Vishnevsky, whose works celebrated the heroic deeds of the Soviet armed forces and working people and who would place a gun on the table when reading a play aloud.

Bulgakov was then commissioned to write a biography of Molière for the popular market, and the typescript was submitted to the authorities in March 1933. However, it was once again rejected, because Bulgakov, never one to compromise, had adopted an unorthodox means of telling his story, having a flamboyant narrator within the story laying out the known details of Molière's life, but also commenting on them and on the times in which he lived; parallels with modern Soviet times were not hard to find. The censor who rejected Bulgakov's work suggested the project should only be undertaken by a "serious Soviet historian". It was finally published only in 1962, and was one of the writer's first works to be issued posthumously. It is now regarded as a major work, both in content and style.

Acting   In December 1934 Bulgakov made his acting debut for MAT as the judge in an adaptation of Dickens's *Pickwick Papers*, and the performance was universally described as hilarious and brilliant. However, though he obviously had great acting ability, he found the stress and the commitment of performing night after night a distraction from his career as a creative writer. He was still attempting to write plays and other works – such as *Ivan Vasilyevich*, set in the time of Ivan the Terrible – which were rejected by the authorities.

At about this time, Bulgakov proposed a play on the life of Alexander Pushkin, and both Shostakovich and Prokofiev expressed an interest in turning the play into an opera. But then Shostakovich's opera *Lady Macbeth of Mtsensk* was slaughtered in the press for being ideologically and artistically unsound, and Bulgakov's play, which had not even gone into production, was banned in January 1936.

Molière, in a revised form, was passed for performance in late 1935, and premiered by MAT in February 1936. However, it was promptly savaged by the newspaper *Pravda* for its "falsity", and MAT immediately withdrew it from the repertoire. Bulgakov, bitterly resentful at the theatre's abject capitulation, resigned later in the year, and swiftly joined the famous Moscow Bolshoi Opera Theatre as librettist and adviser. In November 1936, in just a few hours he churned out *Black Snow* (later to be called *A Theatrical Novel*), a short satire on the recent events at MAT.

Play on Stalin   In mid-1937 he began intensive work on yet another redaction of *The Master and Margarita*, which was finally typed out by June 1938. Soon afterwards, he started work on a play about Stalin, *Batum*. The dictator, although in the main disapproving of the tendency of Bulgakov's works, still found them interesting, and had always extended a certain amount of protection to him. Bulgakov had started work in 1936 on a history of the

USSR for schools and, although the project remained fragmentary, he had gathered a tremendous amount of material on Stalin for the project, which he proposed to incorporate in his play. It is odd that this ruthless dictator and Bulgakov – who was certainly not a supporter of the regime and whose patrician views seemed to date from a previous era – should have been locked in such a relationship of mutual fascination.

Although MAT told him that the play on Stalin would do both him and the theatre good in official eyes, Bulgakov, still contemptuous of the theatre, demanded that they provide him with a new flat where he could work without interruption from noise. MAT complied with this condition. He submitted the manuscript in July 1939, but it was turned down, apparently by the dictator himself.

Bulgakov was devastated by this rejection, and almost immediately began to suffer a massive deterioration in health. His eyesight became worse and worse, he developed appalling headaches, he grew extremely sensitive to light and often could not leave his flat for days on end. All this was the first manifestation of the sclerosis of the kidneys which finally killed him, as it had killed his father. When he could, he continued revising *The Master and Margarita*, but only managed to finish correcting the first part. He became totally bedridden, his weight fell to under fifty kilograms, and he finally died on 10th March 1940. The next morning a call came through from Stalin's office – though not from the leader himself – asking whether it was true the writer was dead. On receiving the answer, the caller hung up with no comment. Bulgakov had had no new work published or performed for some time, yet the Soviet Writers' Union, full of many of the people who had pilloried him so mercilessly over the years, honoured him respectfully. He was buried in the Novodevichy Cemetery, in the section for artistic figures, near Chekhov and Gogol. Ultimately, a large stone which had lain on Gogol's grave, but had been replaced by a memorial bust, was placed on Bulgakov's grave, where it still lies.

Illness and Death

After the Second World War ended in 1945, the country had other priorities than the publication of hitherto banned authors, but Bulgakov's wife campaigned fearlessly for his rehabilitation, and in 1957 *The Days of the Turbins* and his play on the end of Pushkin's life were published, and a larger selection of his plays appeared in 1962. A heavily cut version of *The Master and Margarita* appeared in a specialist

Posthumous Publications and Reputation

literary journal throughout 1966–67, and the full uncensored text in 1973. Subsequently – especially post-Glasnost – more and more works of Bulgakov's were published in uncensored redactions, and at last Western publishers could see the originals of what they had frequently published before in corrupt smuggled variants. Bulgakov's third wife maintained his archive, and both she and his second wife gave public lectures on him, wrote memoirs of him and campaigned for publication of his works. Bulgakov has now achieved cult status in Russia, and almost all of his works have been published in uncensored editions, with unbiased editorial commentary and annotation.

Mikhail Bulgakov's Works

It is difficult to give an overall survey of Bulgakov's works, which, counting short stories and adaptations, approach a total of almost one hundred. Many of these works exist in several versions, as the author revised them constantly to make them more acceptable to the authorities. This meant that published versions – including translations brought out abroad – were frequently not based on what the author might have considered the "definitive" version. In fact to talk of "definitive versions" with reference to Bulgakov's works may be misleading. Furthermore, no new works of his were published after 1927, and they only began to be issued sporadically, frequently in censored versions, from 1962 onwards. Complete and uncut editions of many of the works have begun to appear only from the mid-1990s. Therefore the section below will contain only the most prominent works in all genres.

Themes   Despite the wide variety of settings of his novels – Russia, the Caucasus, Ukraine, Jerusalem in New Testament times and the Paris of Louis XIV – the underlying themes of Bulgakov's works remain remarkably constant throughout his career. Although these works contain a huge number of characters, most of them conform to certain archetypes and patterns of behaviour.

Stylistically, Bulgakov was influenced by early-nineteenth-century classic Russian writers such as Gogol and Pushkin, and he espoused the values of late-nineteenth-century liberal democracy and culture, underpinned by Christian teachings. Although Bulgakov came from an ecclesiastical background, he was never in fact a conventional believer, but, like many agnostic or atheistic Russian nineteenth-century intellectuals and artists, he respected the role that the basic teachings of religion had played in forming Russian and European culture – although they, and Bulgakov, had no liking for the way religions upheld obscurantism and authority.

Some works portray the struggle of the outsider against society, such as the play and narrative based on the life of Molière, or the novel *The Master and Margarita*, in which the outsider persecuted by society and the state is Yeshua, i.e. Jesus. Other works give prominent roles to doctors and scientists, and demonstrate what happens if science is misused and is subjected to Government interference. Those works portraying historical reality, such as *The White Guard*, show the Whites – who were normally depicted in Communist literature as evil reactionaries – to be ordinary human beings with their own concerns and ideals. Most of all, Bulgakov's work is pervaded by a biting satire on life as he saw it around him in the USSR, especially in the artistic world, and there is frequently a "magical realist" element – as in *The Master and Margarita* – in which contemporary reality and fantasy are intermingled, or which show the influence of Western science fiction (Bulgakov admired the works of H.G. Wells enormously).

Bulgakov's major works are written in a variety of forms, including novels, plays and short stories. His first novel, *The White Guard*, was written between 1922 and 1924, but it received numerous substantial revisions later. It was originally conceived as the first volume of a trilogy portraying the entire sweep of the post-revolutionary Civil War from a number of different points of view. Although this first and only volume was criticized for showing events from the viewpoint of the Whites, the third volume would apparently have given the perspective of the Communists. Many chapters of the novel were published separately in literary journals as they appeared. The ending – the dreams presaging disaster for the country – never appeared, because the journal it was due to be printed in, *Rossiya*, was shut down by official order, precisely because it was publishing such material as Bulgakov's. Different pirate versions, with radically variant texts and concocted endings, appeared abroad. The novel only appeared complete in Russian, having been proofread by the author, in 1929 in Paris, where there was a substantial émigré population from the Tsarist Empire/USSR.

The major part of the story takes place during the forty-seven days in which the Ukrainian Nationalists, under their leader

The White Guard

Petlyura, held power in Kiev. The novel ends in February 1919, when Petlyura was overthrown by the Bolsheviks. The major protagonists are the Turbins, a family reminiscent of Bulgakov's own, with a similar address, who also work in the medical profession: many elements of the novel are in fact autobiographical. At the beginning of the novel, we are still in the world of old Russia, with artistic and elegant furniture dating from the Tsarist era, and a piano, books and high-quality pictures on the walls. But the atmosphere is one of fear about the future, and apprehension at the world collapsing. The Turbins' warm flat, in which the closely knit family can take refuge from the events outside, is progressively encroached on by reality. Nikolka Turbin, the younger son, is still at high school and in the cadet corps; he has a vague feeling that he should be fighting on the side of the Whites – that is, the forces who were against both the Nationalists and Communists. However, when a self-sacrificing White soldier dies in the street in Nikolka's arms, he realizes for the first time that war is vile. Near the conclusion of the novel there is a family gathering at the flat, but everything has changed since the beginning of the book: relationships have been severed, and there is no longer any confidence in the future. As the Ukrainian Nationalists flee, they brutally murder a Jew near the Turbins' flat, demonstrating that liberal tolerant values have disintegrated. The novel ends with a series of sinister apocalyptic dreams – indeed the novel contains imagery throughout from the Biblical Apocalypse. These dreams mainly presage catastrophe for the family and society, although the novel ends with the very short dream of a child, which does seem to prefigure some sort of peace in the distant future.

The Life of Monsieur de Molière

The Life of Monsieur de Molière is sometimes classed not as a novel but as a biography. However, the treatment is distinctive enough to enable the work to be ranked as semi-fictionalized. Bulgakov's interpretative view of the French writer's life, rather than a purely historical perspective, is very similar to that in his play on the same theme. The book was written in 1932, but was banned for the same reasons which were to cause problems later for the play. Molière's life is narrated in the novel by an intermediary, a flamboyant figure who often digresses, and frequently comments on the political intrigues of the French author's time. The censors may have felt that the description of the French writer's relationship to an autocrat might have borne too many similarities to Bulgakov's relationship to Stalin.

The book was only finally published in the USSR in 1962, and is now regarded as a major work.

Although he had written fragmentary pieces about the theatre before, Bulgakov only really settled down to produce a longer work on the theme – a short, vicious satire on events in the Soviet theatre – in November 1936, after what he saw as MAT's abject capitulation in the face of attacks by Communists on *Molière*. *A Theatrical Novel* was only published for the first time in the Soviet Union in 1969. There is a short introduction, purporting to be by an author who has found a manuscript written by a theatrical personage who has committed suicide (the reason for Bulgakov's original title, *Notes of the Deceased*; other mooted titles were *Black Snow* and *White Snow*). Not only does Bulgakov take a swipe at censorship and the abject and pusillanimous authorities of the theatre world, but he also deals savagely with the reputations of such people as the theatre director Stanislavsky, who, despite his fame abroad, is depicted – in a thinly veiled portrait – as a tyrannical figure who crushes the individuality and flair of writers and actors in the plays which he is directing. The manuscript ends inconclusively, with the dead writer still proclaiming his wonder at the nature of theatre itself, despite its intrigues and frustrations; the original author who has found the manuscript does not reappear, and it's uncertain whether the point is that the theatrical figure left his memoirs uncompleted, or whether in fact Bulgakov failed to finish his original project.

The Master and Margarita is generally regarded as Bulgakov's masterpiece. He worked on it from 1928 to 1940, and it exists in at least six different variants, ranging from the fragmentary to the large-scale narrative which he was working on at the onset of the illness from which he died. Even the first redaction contains many of the final elements, although the Devil is the only narrator of the story of Pilate and Jesus – the insertion of the Master and Margarita came at a later stage. In 1929 the provisional title was *The Engineer's Hoof* (the word "engineer" had become part of the vocabulary of the Soviet demonology of the times, since in May and June 1928 a large group of mining engineers had been tried for anti-revolutionary activities, and they were equated in the press to the Devil who was trying to undermine the new Soviet society). The last variant written before the author's death was completed around mid-1938, and Bulgakov began proofreading and revising it, making numerous

A Theatrical Novel

The Master and Margarita

corrections and sorting out loose ends. In his sick state, he managed to revise only the first part of the novel, and there are still a certain number of moot points remaining later on. The novel was first published in a severely cut version in 1966–67, in a specialist Russian literary journal, while the complete text was published only in 1973. At one stage, Bulgakov apparently intended to allow Stalin to be the first reader of *The Master and Margarita*, and to present him with a personal copy.

The multi-layered narrative switches backwards and forwards between Jerusalem in the time of Christ and contemporary Moscow. The Devil – who assumes the name Woland – visits Moscow with his entourage, which includes a large talking black cat and a naked witch, and they cause havoc with their displays of magic; however, the epigraph to the novel from Goethe's *Faust* implies that although Woland is the force that works evil, that force will always in the end conduce to good (perhaps an attempt to explain why, if there is a loving God, there is evil in the world) as part of a divine plan.

In the scenes set in modern times, the narrative indirectly evokes the atmosphere of a dictatorship. This is paralleled in the Pilate narrative by the figure of Caesar, who, although he is mentioned, never appears.

The atheists of modern Moscow who, following the contemporary party line, snigger at Christ's miracles and deny his existence, are forced to create explanations for what they see the Devil doing in front of them in their own city.

There are numerous references to literature, and also to music – there are three characters with the names of composers, Berlioz, Stravinsky and Rimsky-Korsakov. Berlioz the composer wrote an oratorio on the theme of Faust, who is in love with the self-sacrificing Margarita; immediately we are drawn towards the idea that the persecuted writer known as the Master, who also has a devoted lover called Margarita, is a modern manifestation of Faust. Bulgakov carried out immense research on studies of ancient Jerusalem and theology, particularly Christology. The novel demands several readings, such are the depths of interconnected details and implications.

Days of the Turbins

Apart from novels, another important area for Bulgakov to channel his creative energy into was plays. *The Days of the Turbins* was the first of his works to be staged: it was commissioned by the Moscow Arts Theatre in early 1925, although it seems Bulgakov had already thought of the possibility of a stage adaptation of *The White Guard*, since acquaintances report him making drafts for such a project slightly earlier. It had an extremely complex history, which involved numerous rewritings after constant negotiations between the writer, theatre, secret police and censors. Bulgakov did not want to leave any elements of the novel out, but on his reading the initial manuscript at the Moscow Arts Theatre it was found to be far too long, and so he cut out a few of the minor characters and pruned the dream sequences in the novel. However, the background is still the same – the Civil War in Kiev after the Bolshevik Revolution. The family are broadly moderate Tsarists in their views, and therefore are anti-Communist but, being ethnically Russian, have no sympathy with the Ukrainian Nationalists either, and so end up fighting for the White Guards. Their flat at the beginning is almost Chekhovian in its warmth, cosiness and air of old-world culture, but by the end one brother has been killed in the fighting and, as the sounds of the 'Internationale' offstage announce the victory of the Communists, a feeling of apprehension grips the family as their world seems to be collapsing round them. The final lines of the play communicate these misgivings (Nikolka: "Gentlemen, this evening is a great prologue to a new historical play." / Studzinsky: "For some a prologue – for others an epilogue."). The final sentence may be taken as representing Bulgakov's fear about the effect the Communist takeover might have on the rest of his own career.

The Soviet playwright Viktor Nekrasov, who was in favour of the Revolution, commented that the play was an excellent recreation of that time in Kiev, where he had also been participating in the historic events on the Bolshevik side – the atmosphere was all very familiar, Nekrasov confirmed, and one couldn't help extending sympathy to such characters as the Turbins, even if they were on the other side: they were simply individuals caught up in historical events.

At around the time of the writing of *The Days of the Turbins*, another Moscow theatre, the Vakhtangov, requested a play from Bulgakov, so he provided them with *Zoyka's Apartment*, which had been first drafted in late 1925. Various alterations had to be made before the censors were satisfied. At least four different texts of *Zoyka* exist, the final revision completed as late as

Zoyka's Apartment

A DOG'S HEART

1935; this last is now regarded as the authoritative text, and is
that generally translated for Western editions.

The setting is a Moscow apartment run by Zoyka; it operates as a women's dress shop and haute-couturier during the
day, and becomes a brothel after closing time. At the time the
play was written, various brothels and drug dens had been
unearthed by the police in the capital, some run by Chinese
nationals. Bulgakov's play contains therefore not only easily
recognizable political and social types who turn up for a
session with the scantily clad ladies, but also stereotypical
Chinese drug dealers and addicts. Zoyka is however treated with
moral neutrality by the author: she operates as the madam of
the brothel in order to raise money as fast as possible so that
she can emigrate abroad with her husband, an impoverished
former aristocrat, who is also a drug addict. In the final act the
ladies and clients dance to decadent Western popular music,
a fight breaks out and a man is murdered. The play ends with
the establishment being raided by "unknown strangers", who
are presumably government inspectors and the police. At this
point the final curtain comes down, so we never find out the
ultimate fate of the characters.

The Crimson Island

In 1924 Bulgakov had written a rather unsubtle short story,
The Crimson Island, which was a parody of the crude agitprop
style of much of the literature of the time, with its stereotypical heroic and noble Communists, and evil reactionaries and
foreigners trying to undermine the new Communist state, all
written in the language of the person in the street – often as
imagined by educated people who had no direct knowledge of
this working-class language. In 1927 he adapted this parody for
the stage. The play bears the subtitle: *The Dress Rehearsal of
a Play by Citizen Jules Verne in Gennady Panfilovich's theatre,
with music, a volcanic eruption and English sailors: in four acts,
with a prologue and an epilogue*. The play was much more successful than the story. He offered it to the Kamerny ["Chamber"]
Theatre, in Moscow, which specialized in mannered and elegant
productions, still in the style of the late 1890s; it was passed
for performance and premiered in December 1928, and was a
success, though some of the more left-wing of the audience and
critics found it hard to swallow. However, the critic Novitsky
wrote that it was an "interesting and witty parody, satirizing
what crushes artistic creativity and cultivates slavish and absurd
dramatic characters, removing the individuality from actors

152

and writers and creating idols, lickspittles and panegyrists". The director of the play, Alexander Tairov, claimed that the work was meant to be self-criticism of the falsity and crudeness of some revolutionary work. Most reviews found it amusing and harmless, and it attracted good audiences. However, there were just a few vitriolic reviews; Stalin himself commented that the production of such a play underlined how reactionary the Kamerny Theatre still was. The work was subsequently banned by the censor in March 1929.

The Crimson Island takes the form of a play within a play: the prologue and epilogue take place in the theatre where the play is to be rehearsed and performed; the playwright – who, although Russian, has taken the pen name Jules Verne – is progressive and sensitive, but his original work is increasingly censored and altered out of all recognition. The rest of the acts show the rewritten play, which has now become a crude agitprop piece. The play within *Crimson Island* takes place on a sparsely populated desert island run by a white king and ruling class, with black underlings. There is a volcano rumbling in the background, which occasionally erupts. The wicked foreigners are represented by the English Lord and Lady Aberaven, who sail in on a yacht crewed by English sailors who march on singing 'It's a Long Way to Tipperary'. During the play the island's underlings stage a revolution and try unsuccessfully to urge the English sailors to rebel against the evil Lord and Lady. However, they do not succeed, and the wicked aristocrats sail away unharmed, leaving the revolutionaries in control of the island.

Bulgakov's play *Escape* (also translated as *Flight*), drafted between 1926 and 1928, and completely rewritten in 1932, is set in the Crimea during the conflicts between the Whites and Reds in the Civil War after the Revolution.

Escape

The Whites – who include a general who has murdered people in cold blood – emigrate to Constantinople, but find they are not accepted by the locals, and their living conditions are appalling. One of the women has to support them all by resorting to prostitution. The murderous White general nurses his colleagues during an outbreak of typhus, and feels he has expiated some of his guilt for the crimes he has committed against humanity. He and a few of his colleagues decide to return to the USSR, since even life under Communism cannot be as bad as in Turkey. However, the censors objected that these people were coming back for negative reasons – simply to get away from where they were – and not because they had genuinely come to believe in the Revolution, or had the welfare of the working people at heart.

Molière

Molière was one of Bulgakov's favourite writers, and some aspects of his writing seemed relevant to Soviet reality – for example the character of the fawning, scheming, hypocritical anti-hero of *Tartuffe*. Bulgakov's next play, *Molière*, was about problems faced by the French playwright during the reign of the autocratic monarch Louis XIV. It was written between October and December 1929 and, as seen above, submitted in January 1930 to the Artistic Board of MAT. Bulgakov told them that he had not written an overtly political piece, but one about a writer hounded by a cabal of critics in connivance with the absolute monarch. Unfortunately, despite MAT's optimism, the authorities did not permit a production. In this piece the French writer at one stage, like Bulgakov, intends to leave the country permanently. Late in the play, the King realizes that Molière's brilliance would be a further ornament to his resplendent court, and extends him his protection; however, then this official attitude changes, Molière is once again an outcast, and he dies on stage, while acting in one of his own plays, a broken man. The play's original title was *The Cabal of Hypocrites*, but it was probably decided that this was too contentious.

Bliss and Ivan Vasilyevich

A version of the play *Bliss* appears to have been drafted in 1929, but was destroyed and thoroughly rewritten between then and 1934. Bulgakov managed to interest both the Leningrad Music Hall Theatre and Moscow Satire Theatre in the idea, but they both said it would be impossible to stage because of the political climate of the time, and told him to rewrite it; accordingly he transferred the original plot to the time of Tsar Ivan the Terrible in the sixteenth century, and the new play, entitled *Ivan Vasilyevich*, was completed by late 1935.

The basic premise behind both plays is the same: an inventor builds a time machine (as mentioned above, Bulgakov was a great admirer of H.G. Wells) and travels to a very different period of history: present-day society is contrasted starkly with the world he has travelled to. However, in *Bliss*, the contrasted world is far in the future, while in *Ivan Vasilyevich* it is almost four hundred years in the past. In *Bliss* the inventor accidentally takes a petty criminal and a typically idiotic building manager from his own time to the Moscow of 2222: it is a utopian society, with no police and no denunciations to the authorities. He finally returns to his own time with the criminal and the building manager, but also with somebody from the future who is fed up with the bland and boring conformity of such a paradise (Bulgakov was always sceptical of the idea of any utopia, not just the Communist one).

Ivan Vasilyevich is set in the Moscow of the tyrannical Tsar, and therefore the contrast between a paradise and present reality is not the major theme. In fact, contemporary Russian society is almost presented favourably in contrast with the distant past. However, when the inventor and his crew – including a character from Ivan's time who has been transported to the present accidentally – arrive back in modern Moscow, they are all promptly arrested and the play finishes, emphasizing that, although modern times are an improvement on the distant past, the problems of that remote period still exist in contemporary reality. For all the differences in period and emphasis, most of the characters of the two plays are the same, and have very similar speeches.

Even this watered-down version of the original theme was rejected by the theatres it was offered to, who thought that it would still be unperformable. It was only premiered in the Soviet Union in 1966. Bulgakov tried neutering the theme even further, most notably by tacking on an ending in which the inventor wakes up in his Moscow flat with the music of Rimsky-Korsakov's popular opera *The Maid of Pskov* (set in Ivan the Terrible's time) wafting in from offstage, presumably meant to be from a radio in another room. The inventor gives the impression that the events of the play in Ivan's time have all been a dream brought on by the music. But all this rewriting was to no avail, and the play was never accepted by any theatre during Bulgakov's lifetime.

In January 1931 Bulgakov signed a contract with the Leningrad Red Theatre to write a play about a "future world"; he also offered it, in case of rejection, to the Vakhtangov Theatre, which had premiered *Zoyka's Apartment*. However, it was banned even before rehearsals by a visiting official from the censor's department, because it showed a cataclysmic world war in which Leningrad was destroyed. Bulgakov had seen the horror of war, including gas attacks, in his medical service, and the underlying idea of *Adam and Eve* appears to be that all war is wrong, even when waged by Communists and patriots.

The play opens just before a world war breaks out; a poison gas is released which kills almost everybody on all sides. A

Adam and Eve

scientist from the Communist camp develops an antidote, and wishes it to be available to everybody, but a patriot and a party official want it only to be distributed to people from their homeland. The Adam of the title is a cardboard caricature of a well-meaning but misguided Communist; his wife, Eve, is much less of a caricature, and is in love with the scientist who has invented the antidote. After the carnage, a world government is set up, which is neither left- nor right-wing. The scientist and Eve try to escape together, apparently to set up civilization again as the new Adam and Eve, but the sinister last line addressed to them both is: "Go, the Secretary General wants to see you." The Secretary General of the Communist Party in Russia at the time was of course Stalin, and the message may well be that even such an apparently apolitical government as that now ruling the world, which is supposed to rebuild the human race almost from nothing, is still being headed by a dictatorial character, and that the proposed regeneration of humanity has gone wrong once again from the outset and will never succeed.

The Last Days   In October 1934 Bulgakov decided to write a play about Pushkin, the great Russian poet, to be ready for the centenary of his death in 1937. He revised the original manuscript several times, but submitted it finally to the censors in late 1935. It was passed for performance, and might have been produced, but just at this time Bulgakov was in such disfavour that MAT themselves backtracked on the project.

Bulgakov, as usual, took an unusual slant on the theme: Pushkin was never to appear on stage during the piece, unless one counts the appearance at the end, in the distance, of his body being carried across stage after he has been killed in a duel. Bulgakov believed that even a great actor could not embody the full magnificence of Pushkin's achievement, the beauty of his language and his towering presence in Russian literature, let alone any of the second-rate hams who might vulgarize his image in provincial theatres. He embarked on the project at first with a Pushkin scholar, Vikenty Veresayev. However, Veresayev wanted everything written strictly in accordance with historical fact, whereas Bulgakov viewed the project dramatically. He introduced a few fictitious minor characters, and invented speeches between other characters where there is no record of what was actually said. Many events in Pushkin's life remain unclear, including who precisely engineered the duel between the army officer d'Anthès and the dangerously liberal thinker Pushkin, which resulted in the writer's death: the army, the Tsar or others? Bulgakov, while studying all the sources assiduously, put his own gloss and interpretation on these unresolved issues. In the end, Veresayev withdrew from the project in protest. The play was viewed with disfavour by critics and censors, because it implied that it may well have been the autocratic Tsar Nicholas I who was behind the events leading up to the duel, and comparison with another autocrat of modern times who also concocted plots against dissidents would inevitably have arisen in people's minds.

The Last Days was first performed in war-torn Moscow in April 1943, by MAT, since the Government was at the time striving to build up Russian morale and national consciousness in the face of enemy attack and invasion, and this play devoted to a Russian literary giant was ideal, in spite of its unorthodox perspective on events.

Commissioned by MAT in 1938, *Batum* was projected as a play about Joseph Stalin, mainly concerning his early life in the Caucasus, which was to be ready for his sixtieth birthday on 21st December 1939. Its first title was *Pastyr* ["The Shepherd"], in reference to Stalin's early training in a seminary for the priesthood, and to his later role as leader of his national "flock". However, although most of Bulgakov's acquaintances were full of praise for the play, and it passed the censors with no objections, it was finally rejected by the dictator himself.

Batum

Divided into four acts, the play covers the period 1898–1904, following Stalin's expulsion from the Tiflis (modern Tbilisi) Seminary, where he had been training to be an Orthodox priest, because of his anti-government activity. He is then shown in the Caucasian town of Batum organizing strikes and leading huge marches of workers to demand the release of imprisoned workers, following which he is arrested and exiled to Siberia. Stalin escapes after a month and in the last two scenes resumes the revolutionary activity which finally led to the Bolshevik Revolution under Lenin. Modern scholars have expressed scepticism as to the prominent role that Soviet biographers of Stalin's time ascribed to his period in Batum and later, and Bulgakov's play, although not disapproving of the autocrat, is objective, and far from the tone of the prevailing hagiography.

Varying explanations have been proposed as to why Stalin rejected the play. Although this was probably because it portrayed the dictator as an ordinary human being, the theory has been advanced that one of the reasons Stalin was fascinated by Bulgakov's works was precisely that the writer refused to knuckle under to the prevailing ethos, and Stalin possibly wrongly interpreted the writer's play about him as an attempt to curry favour, in the manner of all the mediocrities around him.

One Western commentator termed the writing of this play a "shameful act" on Bulgakov's part; however, the author was now beginning to show signs of severe ill health, and was perhaps understandably starting at last to feel worn down both mentally and physically by his lack of success and the constant struggle to try to make any headway in his literary career, or even to earn a crust of bread. Whatever the reasons behind the final rejection of *Batum*, Bulgakov was profoundly depressed by it, and it may have hastened his death from the hereditary sclerosis of the kidneys which he suffered from.

Bulgakov also wrote numerous short stories and novellas, the most significant of which include 'Diaboliad', 'The Fatal Eggs' and *A Dog's Heart*.

Diaboliad

'Diaboliad' was first published in the journal *Nedra* in 1924, and then reappeared as the lead story of a collection of stories under the same name in July 1925; this was in fact the last major volume brought out by the author during his lifetime in Russia, although he continued to have stories and articles published in journals for some years. In theme and treatment the story has reminiscences of Dostoevsky and Gogol.

The "hero" of the tale, a minor ordering clerk at a match factory in Moscow, misreads his boss's name – Kalsoner – as *kalsony*, i.e. "underwear". In confusion he puts through an order for underwear and is sacked. It should be mentioned here that both he and the boss have doubles, and the clerk spends the rest of the story trying to track down his boss through an increasingly nightmarish bureaucratic labyrinth, continually confusing him with his double; at the same time he is constantly having to account for misdemeanours carried out by his own double, who has a totally different personality from him, and is a raffish philanderer. The clerk is robbed of his documents and identity papers, and can no longer prove who he is – the implication being that his double is now the real him, and that he doesn't exist any longer. Finally, the petty clerk, caught up in a Kafkaesque world of bureaucracy and false appearances, goes mad and throws himself off the roof of a well-known Moscow high-rise block.

The Fatal Eggs

'The Fatal Eggs' was first published in the journal *Nedra* in early 1925, then reissued as the second story in the collection

Diaboliad, which appeared in July 1925. The title in Russian contains a number of untranslatable puns. The major one is that a main character is named "Rokk", and the word "rok" means "fate" in Russian, so "fatal" could also mean "belonging to Rokk". Also, "eggs" is the Russian equivalent of "balls", i.e. testicles, and there is also an overtone of the "roc", i.e. the giant mythical bird in the *Thousand and One Nights*. The theme of the story is reminiscent of *The Island of Doctor Moreau* by H.G. Wells. However, Bulgakov's tale also satirizes the belief of the time, held by both scientists and journalists, that science would solve all human problems, as society moved towards utopia. Bulgakov was suspicious of such ideals and always doubted the possibility of human perfection.

In the story, a professor of zoology discovers accidentally that a certain ray will increase enormously the size of any organism or egg exposed to it – by accelerating the rate of cell multiplication – although it also increases the aggressive tendencies of any creatures contaminated in this manner. At the time, chicken plague is raging throughout Russia, all of the birds have died, and so there is a shortage of eggs. The political activist Rokk wants to get hold of the ray to irradiate eggs brought from abroad, to replenish rapidly the nation's devastated stock of poultry. The professor is reluctant, but a telephone call is received from "someone in authority" ordering him to surrender the ray. When the foreign eggs arrive at the collective farm, they look unusually large, but they are irradiated just the same. Soon Rokk's wife is devoured by an enormous snake, and the country is plagued by giant reptiles and ostriches which wreak havoc. It turns out that a batch of reptile eggs was accidentally substituted for the hens' eggs. Chaos and destruction ensue, creating a sense of panic, during which the professor is murdered. The army is mobilized unsuccessfully, but – like the providential extermination of the invaders by germs in Wells's *The War of the Worlds* – the reptiles are all wiped out by an unexpected hard summer frost. The evil ray is destroyed in a fire.

A Dog's Heart was begun in January 1925 and finished the following month. Bulgakov offered it to the journal *Nedra*, who told him it was unpublishable in the prevailing political climate; it was never issued during Bulgakov's lifetime. Its themes are reminiscent of *The Island of Doctor Moreau*, *Dr Jekyll and Mr Hyde* and *Frankenstein*. *A Dog's Heart*

In the tale, a doctor, Preobrazhensky ["Transfigurative", or "Transformational"] by name, transplants the pituitary glands and testicles from the corpse of a moronic petty criminal and thug into a dog (Sharik). The dog gradually takes on human form, and turns out to be a hybrid of a dog's psyche and a criminal human being. The dog's natural affectionate nature has been swamped by the viciousness of the human, who has in his turn acquired the animal appetites and instincts of the dog. The monster chooses the name Polygraf ["printing works"], and this may well have been a contemptuous reference to the numerous printing presses in Moscow churning out idiotic propaganda, appealing to the lowest common denominator in terms of intelligence and gullibility. The new creature gains employment, in keeping with his animal nature, as a cat exterminator. He is indoctrinated with party ideology by a manipulative official, and denounces numerous acquaintances to the authorities as being ideologically unsound, including his creator, the doctor. Although regarded with suspicion and warned as to his future behaviour, the doctor escapes further punishment. The hybrid creature disappears, and the dog Sharik reappears; there is a suggestion that the operation has been reversed by the doctor and his faithful assistant, and the human part of his personality has returned to its original form – a corpse – while the canine characteristics have also reassumed their natural form. Although the doctor is devastated at the evil results of his experiment, and vows to renounce all such researches in future, he appears in the last paragraph already to be delving into body parts again. The implication is that he will never be able to refrain from inventing, and the whole sorry disaster will be repeated ad infinitum. Again, as with 'The Fatal Eggs', the writer was voicing his suspicion of science and medicine's interference with nature, and his scepticism as to the possibility of utopias.

Notes on Shirt Cuffs From 1920 to 1921, Bulgakov worked in a hospital in the Caucasus, where he produced a series of sketches detailing his experiences there. The principal theme is the development of a writer amid scenes of chaos and disruption. An offer was made to publish an anthology of the sketches in Paris in 1924, but the project never came to fruition.

A Young Doctor's Notebook *A Young Doctor's Notebook* was drafted in 1919, then published mainly in medical journals between 1925–27. It is different in nature from Bulgakov's most famous works, being a first-person account of his experiences of treating peasants in his country practice, surrounded by ignorance and poverty, in a style reminiscent of another doctor and writer, Chekhov. Bulgakov learns by experience that often in this milieu what he has learnt in medical books and at medical school can seem useless, as he delivers babies, treats syphilitics and carries out amputations. The work is often published with *Morphine*, which describes the experience of a doctor addicted to morphine. This is autobiographical: it recalls Bulgakov's own period in medical service in Vyazma, in 1918, where, to alleviate his distress at the suffering he was seeing, he dosed himself heavily on his own drugs and temporarily became addicted to morphine.

Select Bibliography

Biographies:
Drawicz, Andrzey, *The Master and the Devil*, tr. Kevin Windle (New York, NY: Edwin Mellen Press, 2001)
Haber, Edythe C., *Mikhail Bulgakov: The Early Years* (Cambridge, MS: Harvard University Press, 1998)
Milne, Lesley, *Mikhail Bulgakov: A Critical Biography* (Cambridge: Cambridge University Press, 1990)
Proffer, Ellendea, *Bulgakov: Life and Work* (Ann Arbor, MI: Ardis, 1984)
Proffer, Ellendea, *A Pictorial Biography of Mikhail Bulgakov* (Ann Arbor, MI: Ardis, 1984)
Wright, A. Colin, *Mikhail Bulgakov: Life and Interpretation* (Toronto, ON: University of Toronto Press, 1978)

Letters, Memoirs:
Belozerskaya-Bulgakova, Lyubov, *My Life with Mikhail Bulgakov*, tr. Margareta Thompson (Ann Arbor, MI: Ardis, 1983)
Curtis, J.A.E., *Manuscripts Don't Burn: Mikhail Bulgakov: A Life in Letters and Diaries* (London: Bloomsbury, 1991)
Vozdvizhensky, Vyacheslav, ed., *Mikhail Bulgakov and his Times – Memoirs, Letters*, tr. Liv Tudge (Moscow: Progress Publishers, 1990)

ALMA CLASSICS

ALMA CLASSICS aims to publish mainstream and lesser-known European classics in an innovative and striking way, while employing the highest editorial and production standards. By way of a unique approach the range offers much more, both visually and textually, than readers have come to expect from contemporary classics publishing.

LATEST TITLES PUBLISHED BY ALMA CLASSICS

To order any of our titles and for up-to-date information about our current and forthcoming publications, please visit our website on:

www.almaclassics.com